LOCALLY LOVE
A RELOCATED CHRISTMASTIME NOVELLA

LORI THORN

ILLUSTRATED BY
HEATHER BALCEREK

This book is dedicated to everyone who's ever enjoyed the feeling of a warm mug in your hands on a cold day.

CHAPTER
ONE

"Oh the fire is slowly dying. And, my dear, we're still good-bye-ing. But as long as you love me so, let it snow, let it snow, let it snow."

"Wake up, sleepy head." Sam brushed Hazel's hair out of the way and kissed her cheek.

Hazel grumbled. "It's too early!" but she rolled out of bed anyway. She pulled on her black running leggings and the pumpkin pie patterned knee-high socks she had purchased for the occasion. "Sam!" She called out to the kitchen.

"Yeah?"

"Where are the turkey hats?"

Sam appeared in the doorway. He was fully dressed in his own running gear; orange shorts (despite the freezing weather), a long-sleeved Turkey Trot technical shirt that came with their entry to the 5k, and a brown and red tutu. "Do you mean these turkey hats?" He presented his hand from behind his back, revealing what looked like a roasted turkey complete with drumsticks on the side and another hat fashioned after a live turkey with a tail on the back.

"Those are the ones!" She sat on the bed to lace her sneakers which were also turkey themed. "Remember when you gave these to me?"

"Of course I do. Your first race. My first gift to you."

"Plus, the whole traveling across the country heroically without even knowing my address." Hazel grinned. "It's been a wild year!"

Sam nodded, a reflective look in his eye. "It's been the best year."

"If we're going to find parking, we'd better go." Hazel grabbed the coffee thermoses and the remaining tutus from the kitchen counter, and they climbed into the car. She smiled at their home as Sam backed out of the drive. When Sam had decided to make the move to Crestwood permanent, it had become quickly apparent that they required a bigger place. Hazel bid farewell to the cozy rental home she loved, and they bought a place in Asheboro, a town on the outskirts of Crestwood. She missed being able to cycle into town but had to admit everything else was quite the upgrade! The outside of their home was light blue with white trim and shutters, but the front door was dark red in contrast. There were azaleas planted along the frontage and maple trees in the yard, so no matter what season it was, the place was beautiful.

Most importantly, they each had their own office to work from. They both continued to thrive in their careers with FutureApp, but that same success made sharing an office space difficult. They couldn't take meetings simultaneously, or they'd be talking over each other. They'd gotten by for a few months by taking turns relocating their laptops to the kitchen table anytime they had overlapping events. Still, it was dysfunctional to be disrupted that much.

Sam pulled into the parking garage in downtown

Crestwood. "Still plenty of spaces. Do you know where we're meeting Nick and Rosie?"

"I'm going to text them when we're down by the starting line so I can tell her where we are exactly."

They took the easiest path to the race, exiting the back of the garage. Hazel stopped in her tracks as they stepped outside. "Oh my god, no way!" Snow gently drifted through the bare tree branches to the ground. She turned to Sam. "This is beautiful!" He took her hand and twirled her around. "You're going to freeze!" She punched his arm.

Sam chuckled, "I won't freeze, I promise!"

"You two are literally disgusting!" Rosie stormed down the hill, apparently having walked around the parking garage. Nick trailed right behind her. "You're dancing in the snow at 6:30 in the morning! It's cold!" She continued to walk straight into Hazel, and they hugged.

Hazel waved at Nick. "You forgot how to winter, staying in Hawaii so long."

Rosie looked into the distance, eyes unfocused. "I want to go back to there."

Sam and Nick clapped each other on the back, and Sam asked, "Yeah, how was the rest of your honeymoon, anyway?"

Rosie and Nick had decided to celebrate their 10th wedding anniversary by renewing their vows in Hawaii and taking the dream vacation they couldn't afford the first time around. Hazel and Sam flew out for a week to be at the vow renewal, but Rosie and Nick stayed on the islands for an entire month.

Nick focused dreamily on Rosie. "It was the absolute best. Best vacation. Best decision to take it we've ever made."

Rosie interjected, "There was this Peace Sanctuary garden on the Big Island that you've got to see. Hazel, you would love it! Plus, all the different sand beaches- black, red, pink! Maybe when you two tie the knot, you can honeymoon there… and take me with you." They all laughed.

"Oh, I nearly forgot!" Hazel handed out the tutus to her friends and shimmied on her own.

Nick noted, "When you said you were bringing these and told us to wear goofy hats, I thought it was strange, but now, as we're surrounded by people dressed as actual turkeys, I understand."

"Are those firefighters here to fight a fire or run?" Rosie pointed to a group of 10 Crestwood Firefighters in their full gear.

"They do the Turkey Trot like that every year. The worst part is they carry all that equipment, and I guarantee they'll wipe the floor with us." Hazel shook her head.

Sam squeezed her shoulder. "You're a much better runner this year; maybe you'll beat them!"

"Well," Hazel shrugged, "I'm much better compared to maintaining the pace of a slug!"

The air horn sounded, and the throng of people slowly began to move along the course. After the first half mile, the crowd started to thin out, the distance between faster and slower runners taking effect. Hazel felt good. She smirked, recalling the same race last year and how she was out of breath by this point.

Beside her, Rosie was letting off a long stream of curses under her breath. "I can't believe you talked me into this."

"Come on, it's fun, right? I never thought I'd like it either, but I'm a total convert."

They finished the first mile, and Rosie wheezed, "I gotta walk for a minute!"

Hazel slowed down next to her and made to shout at Sam, but he was already pulling ahead, Nick on his heels. "I'll walk with you."

Rosie watched the men run out of sight. "Good, they're gone. I've got to tell you something." She was suddenly not at all winded. She remained face forward, walking swiftly and purposefully. Hazel had to increase her pace to keep up.

"Wha-" Hazel began.

"I'm pregnant."

Hazel came to a sudden grinding halt. Runners behind her knocked into her shoulder as they passed and shouted apologies. Rosie was five feet ahead before she realized she was alone. She stopped and gestured for Hazel to catch up.

"I… I don't know what to say." Hazel hissed. "Is this... I guess... How do you feel?"

"I don't know. We decided a long time ago we didn't want kids. We tease each other about it sometimes, but Nick even had a vasectomy because we were sure. It's like some fucking stupid miracle that I'm pregnant. It shouldn't be possible!" Rosie had stopped this time and threw her hands in the air.

Hazel grabbed one and pulled her to the curb, "Let's sit here for a minute." The curb was ice cold and damp from the snow which continued to fall. "What do you want to do?"

Rosie cradled her head in her hands and spoke to her shoes, "The thing is, I never wanted this. We never wanted this. But now that it's happened. I don't know, I feel kind of… happy." Hazel watched Rosie; she didn't *look* happy. "I hate myself for it. It's like I'm betraying Nick. I shouldn't feel good; I shouldn't want this."

Dawning broke over Hazel. "You haven't told Nick."

Rosie finally lifted her head to meet Hazel's eyes. Tears streamed down her cheeks. "You're the only one who knows. I'm so scared, and I've never kept anything from Nick, and it feels horrible." Hazel scooted closer to Rosie and wrapped her in a firm embrace. They stayed there, swaying slightly momentarily, runners thudding past them.

"You two are going to figure this out. You're like the couple everyone aspires to be; I have no doubt you've got this." Hazel paused. "You have to tell him. You'll feel so much better after telling him, and then you'll do what you always do and figure out what's next."

Hazel felt Rosie nod her head. She sniffled. "I know."

Hazel stood and offered a hand to Rosie to help her up. "We've got to get out of this cold first."

They jogged in silence, though Hazel's head pounded with thoughts. When she knew they were approaching the finish line, she said, "There are years worth of evidence that Nick adores you and you're great partners, but I saw him last month at your ceremony. The way he looks at you. It's like you're the sole person in the world. I don't think he even knew he was on a beach! He loves you. Even if you change your mind, even when unexpected things happen."

"I THINK we lost the girls. I didn't realize they were this far back." Sam and Nick stood beyond the inflatable finish line archway, watching other runners pass.

Nick's stomach rumbled audibly. "I'm starving. Let's get in line for some of the bananas. We can also pick up something for them; then, they won't have to wait."

Sam nodded. "Good idea. Plus, I can finally let you know… but you can't tell anyone." Sam shot a sidelong glance at Nick and found him returning a raised eyebrow. They had become fast friends over the past year.

"You know I have to tell Rosie."

Sam grimaced. He loved Rosie, too, and wouldn't usually object, but this had to remain under wraps, and he thought she might struggle to keep it from Hazel. "I don't know. I hate asking you to keep anything from her, but she *can't* say anything to Hazel."

Nick grabbed Sam's arm. "No way!"

A smile erupted across Sam's face. "Yes, way."

"Holy shit, dude!" Nick hugged him. "Welcome to the family officially, I guess! When are you going to do it?"

They inched up the line and snagged protein bars, oranges, and half bananas. "I've got it all planned out. You know the annual gingerbread display at the Grove Park Inn?"

Nick grabbed four waters at the end of the line and used his shirt as a hammock to help carry the loot. "Yeah, of course."

"She thinks we're going on a date to see it. She doesn't know I have a reservation at the restaurant and a room for the night too. We have spa access and room service. The whole thing."

Nick nodded in impressed approval. "Snazzy. She'll love that. What about the ring?"

"Mmm, I did so much research. I never anticipated knowing this much about diamonds and bands. I knew she wouldn't want a blood diamond. I thought about going with another stone altogether, but there are parts of Hazel that are traditional and parts that aren't. I wanted her ring to be the same. I ended up ordering one custom with a princess-cut lab-made diamond. It's simple, but it comes with a unique band with a leafy filigree."

They moseyed back to the finish line, talking and high-fived Hazel and Rosie as they passed through.

"I can't believe it's our first Thanksgiving in our house!" Sam diced onions at the kitchen island.

Hazel worked on the other side, cutting loaves of bread into cubes. "The first holiday season, even! I've been thinking about how we want to decorate. Where will the tree go?"

They looked at each other and laughed. Sam said, "I didn't realize we'd both be so emotional about this!" He carefully tugged his sleeve over his hand and wiped the tears from his eyes.

Hazel used the back of her hand to do the same and quipped, "It's just like someone's cutting onions in here!"

More laughter. "It's *exactly* like that." They mixed the stuffing ingredients and set them aside to be baked later. Sam ticked off items on their list. "Stuffing is prepped, yams are yammed, cranberry sauce is cooling. We've got the quinoa ready to go into the acorn squash, and Rosie and Nick have the bird on lock. I think the last thing we can do is get the pie going!"

Hazel opened a drawer and brandished the rolling pin in the air. "I got you. Let's go."

They were still bustling about the kitchen doing last-minute prep work when the doorbell rang. Hazel peeked at her phone, which displayed a video feed of the front step anytime it detected motion. "It's them."

Nick and Rosie entered carrying a cooked turkey and several bags, which they unloaded in the kitchen. Hazel leaned against a counter chatting with the new arrivals but, after a couple minutes, noticed Rosie making an urgent expression directed solely at her. She struggled to understand what Rosie was trying to communicate and silently mouthed, "What?" Rosie rolled her head toward Nick, still unpacking the canvas shopping bags. He was currently lining up bottles of wine they had brought. "Oh!"

Sam and Nick regarded Hazel. She had exclaimed aloud. She searched her mind for anything to explain her outburst. "Is that a… a Pinot Grigio there? I can't remember the name." She walked to the counter while putting together a plan. Hazel inspected the bottle of white, "Yes, I've actually been wanting to try this for so long!"

Sam shot her an incredulous stare.

Nick replied, "I thought you usually preferred red: what a lucky coincidence."

"You're right, I do, I've just been in the mood for a Grigio, and this one intrigued me."

Sam and Nick resumed their talk, and Hazel turned back to Rosie with a wide-eyed grimace and shrugging shoulders.

All the food prepared, they sat around the circular table and held hands while they reflected on what they felt grateful for. Sam asked to go first. "This has been, hands down, the best year of my life so far. I didn't know relationships like ours could exist, and here we are at the table, sharing with friends who have also found it."

Hazel was next. "Oh no, how do I follow that?" They all chuckled. "I guess, first off, I couldn't agree more, and I'll add that I'm so grateful to be working in Training. Even though it's been bumpy learning a new role at times, it's more fulfilling for me, and I'm enjoying it so much."

Rosie said, "I'm so grateful for Hawaii." They again chuckled, but she insisted, "No, I'm for real. That trip was so needed. Not only did we get to celebrate how far we've come and renew our commitment to each other, but having time in such a beautiful place... It was cleansing. And... And I'm grateful for what's to come, too." Hazel squeezed Rosie's hand.

Nick was last and shared Hazel's sentiment of being difficult to add. "Not to cop out, because truly I have such a sense of gratitude for everything mentioned. I'm grateful for all of you, and cheers to us all!" He led their raising of glasses. After the clink, Hazel watched Rosie pretend to drink from her glass. She positioned it almost right against Hazel's when she set it down.

As the evening progressed, Hazel alternated which glass she drank from. Her plan was working nicely, Rosie had cottoned on right away, and neither of the men seemed to notice their game. Problems didn't begin until she was into what would have been her fourth pour. She was aware of the brain fuzzing of inebriation kicking in. Not good. There had already been an awkward moment requiring her quick thinking when Nick suggested they hit up their favorite sushi restaurant next week, and Rosie kicked her under the table. "I've been in a mood for Mexican lately. Something about their rice. That saffron, am I right?"

To her dismay, Nick and Sam showed no sign of slowing down and refilled their glasses on cue. She kept reminding herself they were only two glasses in, and it was a holiday. They'd be here all night. She needed to speed this along somehow. "Cards Against Humanity with dessert, anyone?"

Sam started clearing the table, Nick stood to help, and Hazel went to fetch the game. She felt a grab of her wrist and turned a little too fast to look at Rosie. Her vision traveled slower than her head. "Thank you," Rosie whispered.

Hazel tried to slow down her imbibement, but the damage was done. At least she could act a little tipsy after what they thought was her third glass. As they played cards, Hazel couldn't decide if Nick was acting strangely or if it was just the booze. There were several moments when she could have sworn he was making faces at Sam, some sort of secretive communication. Then a card was pulled with the prompt 'It was only after marriage that ______ realized ______,' and Nick had exclaimed, "Perfect!" when he slapped it down on the table but then blushed furiously and read the answers with none of his usual gusto.

She made it through several rounds of the game, but Hazel could feel herself falling fast. She needed to sleep. Or vomit. Maybe both. She stood from the table and performed an exaggerated yawn and stretch. "I dunno was wrong wiv me, but I'm soooo tired."

Nick said, "We'll clear out then. You know, guys, craving Mexican and early sleepiness. Be careful; you could be pregnant."

Rosie choked on the water she had sipped and hastily joined them all with an unconvincing titter.

CHAPTER
TWO

"Sweet gingerbread made with molasses, my heart skipped and I reacted."

WHEN HAZEL LOGGED in the Monday after Thanksgiving, she was met with a deluge of incoming emails. "Good grief! Weren't we shut down? Who is emailing over a holiday?!" She frowned at her already empty coffee mug and decided it was a two-cup kind of day.

Sam was in the kitchen when she arrived, laptop opened in the crook of his arm as he poured his first cup. "How are things in Training?"

"No rest for the weary. I just logged in to 106 emails. 106!"

Sam recoiled. "I thought I had it bad with my 65. Maybe they're mostly junk."

Hazel waited to reply until the coffee grinder had finished its job. "I'm sure you're right."

Sam put his computer down and hugged Hazel from behind. "What are you getting into Friday night?"

She smiled and put her hands on top of his. "It's gingerbread time already! I forgot, geez, time is fast after Thanksgiving."

"I'm glad to remind you. I thought it might be fun to dress up a little for it. We haven't gotten gussied in a while."

"Hmmm… Challenge accepted." Hazel spun out of his embrace and finished dressing the Coffee Part Two before returning to her office.

Thankfully, Sam's prediction was correct. Most of her email was automatically generated by system communications. After trudging through them, she reached out to her friends.

Hazel Rogers

How was everyone's Thanksgiving? 9:22am

FRANK SIMMS

Not long enough! 9:22am

MEG MALLOY

They never are smh 9:22am

FRANK SIMMS

> Brian had us in tears. We were going
> around the table saying what we're thankful
> for, and everyone was saying family, friends,
> good job, new house, you know, the normal
> stuff. Brian was last and he goes, "I'm just
> thankful we finally get to eat." 9:23am

Hazel Rogers

> OMG that's hilarious! 9:23am

MEG MALLOY

> The children are always the honest ones
> LOL! He's just saying what everyone else is
> thinking. 9:23am

MEG MALLOY

> Ours was quiet. Just me and Jules this year
> which was honestly so nice. We did the big
> family thing last year, which I appreciate
> too, but I don't know, it felt good to chill this
> year. 9:24am

Hazel Rogers

> I feel you Meg. We had our friends over for the first Thanksgiving in the new house. It was fun. A little weird but fun! 9:24am

FRANK SIMMS

A little weird? Talk more. 9:24am

HAZEL ROLLED HER EYES. She knew Frank would be all over her as soon as she hit send.

MEG MALLOY

Frank you are such a snoop! 9:24am

FRANK SIMMS

Ya'll love me and you know it. 9:24am

Hazel Rogers

I guess I can tell you as there is no chance of you telling anyone else. One of my friends is pregnant and hasn't told her husband yet. It's a long story, but it ends in me drinking way too much and having the worst hangover ever Friday. 9:25am

Frank Simms

YOU DIDN'T! 9:25am

Frank Simms

Tell me you didn't drink all your friend's drinks and yours?! 9:25am

Hazel Rogers

I did. Mistakes were made. 9:26am

Meg Malloy

You pour sweet thing. (See what I did there?) 9:26am

Hazel Rogers

A+ pun work. 9:26am

FRANK SIMMS

That's true friendship right there. 9:27am

HAZEL CHECKED HER CALENDAR. The Training department was transitioning to its quieter quarter. It was the inverse of the rest of the business. Training helped onboard new hires as their longest and biggest push of the year right before the holiday season when things were busiest for the majority of FutureApp. The winter holiday was so focused on customer support, Training wasn't allowed to offer courses until mid-January, so they used the November and December months to plan and prepare for the courses they'd provide throughout the year. This was another perk of Training for Hazel. Winter was the quiet, reflective time in nature, and it was the same in Training. Today's main event was the Looking Forward, an annual meeting where the team would learn how they'd be utilized next year.

There was a lot of discussion in her team chatrooms as the meeting time approached. Anxiety was in the air as people talked about what initiative they hoped they would support (and from some of the more senior people, things they never wanted to support again).

Hazel ensured her appearance was in in order in the camera before clicking to enter the SyncUp, FutureApp's virtual meeting App. Jasmond was already the center of attention, welcoming his team as they streamed in, each person announced with a tinkling chime upon entry.

Once most people were in attendance and settled in, Jasmond flashed his bright smile and called them to attention. "Most of us know how this goes. We'll talk about what we accomplished last year, what we learned, the roadmap for next year, and our assignments."

The first part of the meeting was a slog. It wasn't unimportant information to cover, but they had already covered it. The Training department was accustomed to performing Post Mortem after all their activity, so their wins and losses were common knowledge among the team. Hazel figured they must cover this part as a reminder or for those not in the department. She noted several names she was vaguely familiar with but couldn't place.

Sam Pierce

How's the Look For? 1:31pm

Hazel Rogers

Nothing to report so far, but we should move into more exciting territory soon. 1:31pm

Hazel Rogers

I hope. 1:32pm

As IF HER wish were granted, the next slide Jasmond presented was the roadmap for the year. Hazel found that besides Onboarding, they'd offer classes on Building Financial Acumen, Meeting the Customer, Understanding Today's App Landscape, Leadership Development Series, and two Communications Series; Professional Communication in the Workplace and Communicating with Customers. She had an inkling she would be placed in one of the Communications Series, having recently come from that department. Which would be… okay. Fair. The only one she didn't want was Financial Acumen. Jasmond gave brief descriptions of each. All chatting ended, and Hazel had the impression everyone was holding their breath for what came next.

"I know you've all been waiting for this part. Before we get to assignments, I want to assure you that a lot of consideration has gone into these. I truly believe we've set this up for success at an individual and company level." Jasmond flipped to the next slide, and Hazel's eyes hungrily searched for her name. She found it at the bottom of the page, listed in the assistant position for Communication in the Workplace. Her shoulders slumped. The assistance position? And nothing else? She had been given positive, constructive feedback throughout the year and believed she had performed well, but maybe she hadn't.

Hazel Rogers

I got the assistant trainer position for
Communication in the Workplace Series.
1:54pm

. . .

Sam Pierce

You do have amazing Comms experience
that makes sense to utilize. 1:55pm

Hazel Rogers

Yeah, but as the assistant? It's my whole
assignment. Most other assistants are
doing something in addition. I don't know,
maybe I'm not doing as well as I thought.
It's embarrassing. 1:56pm

Sam appeared at her office door. "Hey."

"Hey." She couldn't bring herself to look at him; she didn't want to cry.

"You're awesome. You are a high performer and would know if you weren't meeting the expectations. Think of every conversation you've had this year."

Hazel knew he was right, but then why would she be given such a light assignment? She took a steadying breath. "You're right. I should just ask about it. Assuming the worst is my go-to, though!" She quipped, suddenly feeling better. "Thank you for the grounding."

Sam winked at her. "I always got you, babe."

Hazel planned to organize her thoughts and request some time with Jasmond later in the day, but he reached out to her first!

Jasmond Merrill

> Hey Hazel, I'm scheduling a meeting with
> you for next week. Didn't want to catch you
> off guard! 3:01pm

Hazel Rogers

> Hey, thanks! I wanted to talk to you also. I
> had some questions about the
> assignments. 3:01pm

Jasmond Merrill

> Yep! We'll discuss more then. See you soon
> :) 3:02pm

Hazel Rogers

> See you then! 3:02pm

SAM WAS PLAYING the most frustrating game of phone tag he'd ever been part of. He needed to talk to Grown Brilliance, the company making Hazel's custom ring, but there were limited times he could do so considering work and that Hazel couldn't overhear the conversation. Morning was out of the question as the busiest part of the day. His lunchtime attempts had been thwarted first by Hazel delivering a surprise egg salad sandwich, then by the answering machine indicating the company was also closed during lunchtime. To their credit, Grown Brilliance also tried to reach Sam but invariably called during a meeting he couldn't step away from or when he and Hazel were together, forcing him to glance at the screen and say, "Spam caller."

Now he was wearing his smartest suit, dark blue slim-fitting pants, and blazer that he'd paired with an off-white colored shirt with thin blue vertical floral patterns. He'd left the collar undone for a more casual appearance and had even buffed his brown leather shoes. Though he'd never gotten connected with them on a call, he knew the answer he was seeking. Hazel's ring must have been delayed. It certainly hadn't arrived, and now it was too late to hope he'd have it in time to propose tonight.

A lot of thought and careful planning had gone into the evening, and Sam was thoroughly annoyed that despite all of it, he wouldn't be able to deliver the perfect moment in his head. His phone rang, and he recognized the number as Grown Brilliance. It was risky, but Hazel was still getting ready in their bedroom. He bottled his irritation and answered the call as quietly as possible.

"Hello, this is Patty from Grown Brilliance calling for Mr. Sam Pierce?"

"Hey Patty, you've got him."

"Sorry for not being able to connect earlier in the week. We did want to let you know that the ring you ordered had an unexpected issue in the original creation run which has delayed our expected delivery. The good news is we do have the ring now, it's beautiful, and it will be shipped tomorrow with expected delivery Monday."

Sam massaged his temple. This wasn't anyone's fault, and he couldn't be mad about it, but he was disappointed and almost grieving for the night's loss. "Thanks for the update, Patty. It's good to know the new delivery date."

"You're welcome, Mr. Pierce. If you need anything, just give us a call."

He exhaled sadly and dropped the phone to his side.

"Who was that? Is everything okay?" Hazel was behind him and had clearly noted his body language.

"Oh, yeah, it was the Grove Park Inn. They were letting me know they… That they…" Sam had spun around to face her. "You've got to stop stealing my words!"

Hazel cackled like a cartoon villain. "Har har! I never will!"

"No, you won't. You're too beautiful." Hazel was wearing a shimmering gown of navy that flaunted the curve of her hips. She'd even done her hair up in a twist.

"It isn't too much, is it? You said to dress up."

Sam spun his finger in the air. "Give me a twirl." The bottom of the dress fanned out as she did, and the back traveled up her spine but left her toned shoulders on display. "It's perfect."

"Thank you, you flirt! So, what did the Grove Park want?"

Seeing Hazel had washed all his bitter, disappointed feelings away in a moment. Even without the ring, tonight was going to be great! Whatever they did was always fun and effortless, and right. "Oh, they wanted to let me know our entry time was postponed. I guess one of the groups ahead of us didn't clear out on time."

"Oh, no big deal. Let's go see the GINGERBREAD!" She shouted the word in a heavy metal growl, held her dress aloft, and skipped toward the door.

Arriving at the Grove Park Inn made Hazel imagine what it must be like to cross into another world. Even the road to the Inn was a transformative experience. They drove along a remote mountain road one minute until suddenly, all the trees on either side were swathed in perfect white string lights. "I say this every year, but wow!" Hazel turned her head all around to see the lights better. The drive continued until a sharp right turn revealed the castle-like Inn adorned with enormous wreaths, ribbons, trees, and lights. The parking attendants helped direct them to an open spot, and Hazel and Sam linked arms to walk up the hill to the main entrance.

The receiving room was an enormous hall with the tallest Christmas tree Hazel had ever seen. Two fireplaces were on each side of the room, and people buzzed about, posing for photos in front of the tree and talking merrily. Hazel veered toward the right, knowing the way to the National Gingerbread House Competition displays from years past. Realizing Sam wasn't with her, she turned to see him speaking with the maitre'd. She narrowed her eyes, and his smile overtook his face making his dimple noticeable from across the room. Sam waved for her to join, and they were led into the restaurant.

Hazel had never been in the restaurant before. The tables were set with oversized leather chairs that were spread farther apart from each other than was typical. There were windows stretching from the floor to the high ceiling along the far wall. Excitement thrilled through her when they were led to a window-side table. The view was spectacular. The sunset over the mountains stretched to infinity. "They really do look blue."

Sam pulled her chair out for her. "Because of the trees."

"Huh?"

"It's true! The native trees here release some chemicals and terpenes that create the blue color."

Hazel shook her head. "What is happening right now? You know more about my mountains than I do, and we're sitting at the fanciest restaurant I've ever been to? Unbelievable!"

He shot her an impish grin. "It's my sacred duty to keep you guessing… In a good way."

When the waiter placed the Benne Seed Crusted Sea Bass in front of Hazel, her jaw dropped. She nearly cried when it was as delicious as it looked.

The colors painted across the sky changed from the bright new sunset colors to deeper hues of pink and orange before settling into a velvety night. "Would you like dessert here or in the Great Hall Bar? You can also order in the room until 1am." Hazel startled at the waiter's return; she had been staring out the window, considering ways to repay Sam for this wonderful surprise.

Sam answered for them, "We'll check out the Great Hall. This was incredible. Thank you so much."

The waiter exited, and Hazel raised an eyebrow at Sam. "We will?"

"Well yeah, it's a special night, we could get a cocktail, or I hear they've got a great fruit salad, too, and then walk around the displays."

It was eight days after the wine event of Thanksgiving, and Hazel wasn't entirely ready to drink anything alcoholic yet. "Maybe a coffee would be nice."

"I'm sure that could be arranged." Sam stood up and held his hand out to her.

They strolled leisurely side by side. Even the halls were vast and luxurious. Some had rich oaken sides with wainscoting, art she was sure was worth a fortune along the walls, and plush forest green carpets. Others were built of large rough rocks that gave the impression of being in a cavern; the floors here were also stone but were polished blue hues. Sam seemed to know where they were going, so she let him lead the way. They arrived at an open area with an enormous hearth. The windows were smaller here, and the seating more casual. As they walked to the bar, a pianist sat at the grand piano on the far side of the room and began playing a complicated jazzy number.

Drinks attained, they headed to the gingerbread displays at last. Hazel loved many things about the holiday season, but this was one of the most unique. Each year contestants from around the country entered the National Competition, which was the major league of gingerbreading. The creativity was boundless, and the feats achieved using exclusively edible ingredients were mind-blowing. This year was no different. They saw a working advent calendar, a carousel, a recreation of the Grove Park Inn to scale, two pandas eating bamboo which was more like a painted statue than a dessert cookie, ships, boats, trains, a Santa Sleigh Zeppelin, St. Basil's Cathedral, and countless other entrants.

When they had exhausted the displays, Sam gave her a flirtatious look. He placed his hand on the small of her back, a move he knew drove her feral. "I guess we better get to our room."

Hazel jabbed him with an elbow. "Our room?"

He fished a key from his pocket. "Room 521."

"You sneaky little snake!" She saw his throat bob and felt his gaze travel down her body. "I guess we better find our room, indeed."

On the elevator up, Hazel shot a quick text to Rosie. They messaged frequently, but Hazel intended to be there for her even more now that she needed it.

Hazel

> Hey, just checking in! Gingerbread is good
> this year, how are you? 8:03pm

Rosie

> I think the real question is how are YOU?
> 8:03pm

HAZEL BOGGLED AT THE MESSAGE. Sam must have told
them about the date tonight.

Hazel

> I'm great! Sam planned this spectacular
> date, we're actually staying at the Inn! But I
> guess you knew that already, lol 8:03pm

Rosie

> Okay, I'm doing fine, don't worry about me.
> You stay focused on having a night you'll
> never forget. 8:04pm

THE ELEVATOR DOOR OPENED. Sam knelt down. "Piggyback
to your room for the night?" She gathered her dress and
hugged him around his neck. Hazel felt free and joyful and

giggled down the hall as Sam galloped with her. His mirthful calls in her ear made her heart sing, and she was reminded of another time they met in a hallway. Time had slowed then, too.

A small mechanical click denoted the unlocking of their door, and Sam gently lowered her directly onto the bed. They lay facing each other on their sides. Hazel reached out and caressed his chest. She unbuttoned one button, then the next. "You make me feel like a kid some-times and like a woman, others."

Sam pulled back as if she'd hit him. "When my goal is to make you feel like a kid sometimes and a queen, others?!"

"All I'm saying is it's adult time, whatever the title. You certainly deserve to be treated like a king tonight." Sam pulled his jacket off. Hazel traced her finger down slowly from his shoulder to his chest, along his abs, until she met his pants. Her voice husky, "These have to go." She undid his belt and flung it behind her. She bit her lower lip feeling his erection push against the fly of his pants as she unzipped them. A ravenous sound escaped Hazel as she lowered herself onto the floor before him, bringing his briefs and pants with her.

Hazel swallowed him, the head of his cock pressed against the back of her throat. Sam leaned back, moaning. She hummed to send vibrations through his entire member, and it caused her to gag slightly. She worked in a sequence, first up and down the length of him, swirling her tongue around and around, then using her hand while she flicked and sucked at his frenulum. Sam's cock twitched in her mouth. She suppressed the urge to mount him and slid him inside her mouth as far as she could again while firmly massaging his perineum. Fingers weaved through the hair at the top of Hazel's head and tugged. "I've got to get you out of that dress."

Hazel stood slowly and spun toward the window, her back to Sam. She pulled the clip out of her hair, letting it fall to her shoulders. He swept it aside, kissed her neck, and unzipped her gown. It dropped, crumpling in a circle around her feet with a soft swoosh. "Even without it, you look like the heavens." He caressed her back down to her hips, then picked her up and swung her back to the bed. He was on top of her all in one smooth movement.

Sam rubbed his cock against her clit playfully before sinking into her. Hazel closed her eyes, relishing the connection, feeling like they had become more than themselves. He slowly thrust into her. Too slow. It became maddening, and she scratched his back to urge his tempo. He exclaimed a small "Oh," and responded by picking up the pace. Hazel pulled him against her and teased his nipples until they were hard.

Sam arched back and lifted her right leg, resting it on his shoulder. "I can tell you want it rough tonight."

"Mmm, I do love it when you treat me like a drum. That slapping sound…." Hazel glanced around the room. She hadn't even registered her surroundings when they came through the door. "Take me against the window."

"I'd.. what?" Sam looked in the direction Hazel was turned to.

"We're in a fancy room with a breathtaking view. We should take advantage, right?"

"Your wish is my command."

Their room window also nearly stretched from floor to ceiling. It was pitch outside, but she could see little dots of house light scattered across the mountains in the distance, and stars shone from the sky.

Sam moved an ottoman against the wide window ledge. "Put your knees on this." Hazel knelt on the ottoman and braced her hands on the ledge. "You're right.

This view is stunning." Sam grasped her hips firmly and took her from behind.

Warmth built-in Hazel's chest, a stark contrast from the coolness of the window before her. Sam drove into her, filling her up completely. She searched for something to hold onto but, finding nothing, lowered herself slightly to lean on her forearm. She reached between her legs with the other hand and wrapped her fingers around his dick, feeling it enter her. The warmth in her chest grew at the wet hardness there. Hazel gasped, "Play with my clit." Sam growled, his hand instantly there; hers retreated to help steady herself.

Electricity released through her body like lightning bolts. She came so hard she shook. Behind her, Sam grabbed her hips again and roared. Hazel felt the intensity of his erection increase before his release.

Her whole body fizzled with post-orgasmic euphoria. Hazel fell into the bed and, for the first time, realized how fluffy the blankets were; she sank into them. Sam joined, stroking her hair until she fell asleep.

SAM LEANED against the doorframe to the bathroom brushing his teeth. He wasn't dressed yet, and she enjoyed the shadows on his chiseled obliques. "It's creepy when you watch me sleep," Hazel mumbled. Sam just shrugged.

It wasn't until he spat out the toothpaste that he answered, "You shouldn't be so gorgeous all the time, then. You might want to throw on a robe. Our breakfast is going to be here any minute."

"Room service! I've always wanted room service!"

Sam pulled on a shirt and plopped next to her. "I know."

A feast was spread across their bed in short order. "Did

you order one of everything?" Hazel laughed and dressed her coffee.

"I may have gone a little overboard."

Morning light lifted into their room as they ate their way through omelets, stuffed French toast, berries, and croissants.

Remembering the text from Rosie, Hazel teased Sam, "I can't believe you told Rosie about all this and didn't tell me!"

Sam took a bite of the croissant. "I didn't." His face turned suddenly serious, but the expression didn't quite match the conversation. "I did. Sorry, I forgot." He paused and sipped his coffee before asking, "What'd she say?"

"Nothing, really. She seemed to know we were going to have a great time." Relief washed his face, and she saw his shoulders relax. "Anyway, I need to get in some reading time when we're home. *Santa's Huge Talent* isn't going to read itself."

Sam shook his head. "The title gets me every time. But you'll have to wait a little longer. We haven't even been to the spa yet."

CHAPTER

THREE

"Deck the halls with boughs of holly, fa la la la la, la la la la."

Moving to Asheboro meant she didn't get to enjoy downtown Crestwood nearly as often as she used to. However, Hazel and Rosie still stole away time there whenever they could. Hazel was sitting on a pouf in their favorite section in the back rooms of Chai Chai, the local tea lounge. She'd arrived half an hour early so she could relax and read. Crestwood Book Club had been on hiatus for a couple months due to people being out of town but would resume next week, and Hazel couldn't wait! She also had to admit that *Santa's Huge Talent* was a surprising page-turner. Hazel had picked it out, recalling a conversation from last year where her friend Jessica lamented that the holiday book they were reading probably featured Santa but not his candy cane.

Hazel glanced up when she heard the beaded curtain rattle. Rosie was there and was clearly bursting to tell her

32

something. She wore a puffy vest over a long sleeve purple shirt and jeans and a smile that radiated excitement. She even did a little dance back and forth, which set her ponytail swaying.

"Okay, out with it!" Hazel demanded as Rosie took the pouf next to her. "You obviously have something on your mind."

Rosie cocked her head to the side. She carefully answered. "I do… but what about you?"

"What about me, what?" Hazel chuckled.

"You don't have anything to share?"

"I mean, I was going to tell you about the spa and my meeting next week that I'm a little nervous about at work, but you're practically bursting over there, so please spill first!"

Rosie scrunched her face in a disbelieving way for a flash, but then her brilliant smile returned. "I told him."

"Oh, my God! I can't believe you didn't tell me this already! When did it happen? He obviously took it well? *I told you you'd be fine!* Ah! Tell me everything!"

"It just happened last night. I couldn't take it anymore. At first, I was so scared this would mean the end of our relationship or the end of not only the pregnancy but the dream of having a family that had been planted in my head. The longer it was a secret, the worse I felt because I knew- trust me, I always give this advice to my patients- I *knew* keeping it was wrong, and guilt was eating me alive. Anyway, I was feeling sick, mentally and physically. I was on the couch, and Nick was playing a video game, and I didn't realize I was going to porf until it was too late. I sat up and panicked and said, "I'm going to puke!" Nick dropped his controller and ran to the kitchen to get a bag. He was so fast, and he held my hair back on the couch, and then I started to cry. The words just started coming out. Sort of, because I was crying really hard, but he got the gist. So he was there, holding a bag of my vomit, and Hazel, he was furious. I've never seen Nick so angry."

Hazel squinted. "He was angry? I know this isn't the end because of the delivery." Rosie was still beaming as she recounted the events.

"He was. He turned so red. He even yelled."

"Nick yelled?" This was unheard of.

Rosie nodded emphatically, "He did. He asked how long I knew, and he lost it when I told him a couple of weeks. He asked how I could keep anything like this from him. We never have kept anything from each other. He ran out of the room with the bag, and I stayed on the couch and cried. Then he came back a few minutes later and sat down next to me, and he was crying too, and he asked why I hadn't told him right away. So I told him everything. And Hazel, we were both sniveling blobs at this point; I'm not sure we were even speaking English anymore, but he asked, 'How could you keep the best news I've ever heard from me?'" And now Rosie and Hazel had tears running down their cheeks. "He told me he started having second thoughts about parenthood last year. Your Mom's journal, actually. I guess I said something about keeping one for our kids. I don't even remember it, though I'm sure it was me being snarky. But it made him think, and he thought I'd never go for it, so he didn't say anything."

Hazel's entire face shone from her wiping tears. "I'm so happy for you!" An idea struck her suddenly, and she gasped. "I'm going to be an aunt!"

They held each other until their sniffles subsided, and pulling apart, Rosie smacked Hazel's arm, "Tell me about Grove Park Inn!"

Sam

Dude. 9:09am

Sam

You told her already? 9:09am

Sam

I knew it was only a matter of time, but I thought you'd hold out a little longer lol 9:09am

Nick

Yes, you know how it goes, I did just find she was keeping something pretty huge from me 9:15am

Nick

but how'd you know that I told her? and more importantly, how come we haven't heard about the big event? 9:15am

Sam

You haven't heard anything because it didn't happen. Rings not here yet. And I figured because she mentioned something to Hazel about having a memorable night, which was still true so it's all good. 9:16am

SAM NOTICED the comment about Rosie keeping things from Nick but wasn't sure what to do with it. Asking seemed like prying, and if Nick wanted to explain more, he would... right? Or was he mentioning it because he wanted to be asked?

Sam

I hope everything is okay with you and Rosie. 9:24am

SAM'S PHONE RANG. Nick was FaceTiming him, something they had never done before. He pressed the accept button, and Nick's face appeared on the screen. He said, "I just couldn't text it... but I also couldn't wait to see you in person, and Rosie agreed since she told Hazel, I get to tell you."

Sam had no idea what Nick was talking about, but his bubbly demeanor made him grin. "Okayyyy, so..."

But Nick cut him off, "We're parents! I'm going to be a Dad!"

Sam pumped his fists in the air, whooped, then realized he was videoconferencing and quickly lowered the phone back to his face. "Congratulations! I'm so happy for you both. Do you know the due date?"

"Not officially yet. It's still early, but some back-of-the-napkin math, and it's likely mid-July."

Sam snickered, "Oh, she's going to be fully pregnant when it's hot outside. Bless us all."

Nick looked as if he was imagining it. "Yeah."

"We'll help with all of it," Sam offered, "baby shower, setting up the nursery, babysitting, once that's a thing!"

Nick's attention snapped back to the phone. "They say it takes a village. You two are our village."

The statement, how genuine Nick had said it, hit Sam in the heart. His breath hitched, and he tried to steal his composure. "You don't know how much that means to me." He paused, considering how to explain. "When I moved here, it was the obvious answer. It was such a force of nature; I couldn't have stopped it, even if I had reservations. That doesn't mean it wasn't scary to leave my friends and everything I knew behind. But I left no relationship back in Portland that compares to my friendship with you."

Nick wiped at the corner of his eye and said, "Aw man, Rosie has gotten to both of us with her counseling ways. I think we might be *too* able to express our emotions."

Sam put on a mock Rosie voice, "Ah, but are you feeling your feelings? What part of your body do you feel that in?" They both chuckled. "Yeah, she's got us alright "

HAZEL BOUNCED through the door and sang into the house, "I hope you're ready to decorate!"

A crashing sound answered, followed by, "I'm okay!" Sam was ready to decorate; he'd gotten down all the Christmas boxes from the attic after his conversation with Nick. Hazel popped her head around the doorway to the garage. "Thanks for getting everything down. I'll help carry them in." She grabbed a box so wide she had to tilt it to fit through the doorway.

"How was Chai Chai?"

She let the box drop the last few inches onto the living room floor. "It was great!"

Sam ran his tongue over his teeth. "Mmhmm, and what did you talk about?"

"This and that, you know, normal stuff. Work. I told her about The Grove Park." Sam leaned closer to Hazel, an intense, expectant stare aimed right at her until she finally lifted her gaze to him. "What?"

"Rosie didn't talk to you about… *anything else?*"

Hazel's jaw dropped, and her eyes lit with excitement. "You know! Nick told you?"

"And you apparently already knew?! I can't believe you didn't tell me!"

Hazel gave him an apologetic pout. "I couldn't; Nick didn't even know yet. It was a whole thing."

Sam leaned back on his elbows against the carpet. "I'm only teasing you. I totally get it. But wow, this is going to change so many things. I can't stop thinking about it. Nick is so excited. I wish you could've seen him."

"I know. Rosie, too, couldn't sit still the whole time. There's going to be a baby! I hope you're ready, Uncle Sam."

"Oh no!" Sam felt stunned. "I never realized being an uncle would remind me so much of historic military recruitment."

"Uncle Sammy?" Hazel asked.

Sam shrugged, "I'll recruit them to a life of Corporate Communications. And running!"

Hazel giggled. "Add on cooking and reading!"

They spent the rest of the day decorating the house. The Christmas tree went in front of the living room, and they sang carols with abandon as they strung up white lights and ornaments. Sam put colorful strands of lights along the edges of the roof and windows while Hazel spiraled them around the tree trunks in the front yard.

At sunset, they stood back to admire their work. Hazel leaned against Sam's shoulder. "It looks like a Thomas Kinkade." He kissed the top of her head. If he had the ring, he'd propose right now.

OVER THE YEARS of her employment at FutureApp, Hazel had developed a certain amount of confidence. She even got to know their CEO last year and presented at their annual summit! As she prepared to go into her meeting with Jasmond, however, she was not particularly confident at all. Hazel straightened all the items on her desk and watched the clock, her foot bouncing nervously. She logged into the SyncUp right on time and found Jasmond already there, but muted and clearly talking to someone else. He saw her enter and held up a finger to indicate he'd be with her shortly.

A small pop of his microphone turning on sounded before he apologized. "Sorry about that, Hazel. My kiddo forgot her backpack, and the school called. Going to run it up there as soon as I can."

"No worries!" Hazel grinned. Her nerves waning a bit already. Jasmond tended to have that effect on people. His nature was reassuring and calming.

"Thanks. I know you had questions about your assignments for the year, which I also wanted to talk to you about. I think things will make more sense after I share the complete vision with you, and of course, you're free to ask anything. You already know that, though." She nodded. "What you saw last week is your placement as the assistant trainer for the Communications in the Workplace series. What are your thoughts on that?"

Hazel fidgeted with the pen in her hand. "As soon as I saw the classes, I thought it would be likely I'd be on the Communications ones. It makes sense, given I transferred from Comms recently, but honestly, I thought I'd be on a lead."

Jasmond nodded in exaggerated motions. "That was our first plan, yes. Then something else came across my desk, and I knew you were perfect for it. Let me preemptively say you can say no to this. I realize you just got here after trying to move to Training for a long time, and now, as soon as you're here, I'm trying to loan you out. It's a compliment to you. It's because you're so good." He appraised her for a second. "You thought you were in trouble, didn't you?"

Hazel frowned and shot her eyes left and right before admitting, "Maybe."

"You're too damned humble for your own good!" She smiled and aimed her eyes at the keyboard, trying not to blush. "Alright, let's get to it. Last year you changed our onboarding practices by adding a segment about how to succeed in a remote work environment. Now we want to tackle retention from another angle. Our recruitment team wants to update their hiring profile so we're searching for people more likely to succeed working from home before we even make an offer."

"Oh!" Hazel slapped the desk, "I told Tamra we needed to look at the profile!"

Jasmond chuckled. "I'm sure you did. That's another indication you'd be the best resource to help Recruiting. It is a big assignment. You'd be working with Ted Proctor and his team. Bailey Wendell is the HR person who supports them, and they've also hired a consulting firm to review the entire recruiting process."

Hazel made a sour face. "A consulting firm?"

"Yeah, I know." She'd never seen Jasmond roll his eyes before. It lasted seconds, and he was back in hyper-professional mode. "The other part is they want you to take the Recruitment Training and participate in recruitment for a month so you'll have a little hands-on experience… Can you see why I limited you to an assistant role outside of onboarding? That is, if you want to go this route. You can take a couple days and think about it."

Hazel shook her head. "I don't need a couple days. I'm in. I am so flattered you thought of me for this project."

Jasmond grabbed for his heart and exhaled. "Thank goodness you said yes! I don't have anyone else quite as prepared for something like this. I know you'll do us proud! I'll send over word to Ted, and I'm sure he'll reach out to you soon. Things will be getting started after the new year."

ASHEBORO'S DOWNTOWN was a single street, but Hazel thought it was darling. Street lamps were all wrapped in garland and lights, and the storefronts were equally dressed for the season. Windows were painted with snowmen and candy canes. Inside, displays of wintry wonderlands and decorated trees with wrapped gifts beneath were abound; the holiday spirit was ubiquitous.

Hazel bumped her hip into Sam as they walked beside each other enjoying the festive street. After her eye-opening discussion with Jasmond and her excitement about working with Recruiting mounting all day, she'd asked Sam to go out with her. They were bundled in jackets, and wisps of snow flurries floated around them. Once she had exhausted all the details of her new work assignment, Hazel asked, "Why were you so weird about the mail today?"

Sam glanced at her, his face nearly invisible between his beanie and maroon scarf wrapped up around his chin. "What do you mean?"

"You know what I mean! You must have checked the mailbox five times today!" He put on a show of inspecting a window display and kept his silence. "I know what's happening."

Hazel saw a devious gleam in his deep brown eyes. "Do you?"

"Christmas presents! You could just tell me not to check the mail; I promise I'll behave."

Sam smirked. "You got me there. I'll never believe the behaving bit, though." He grabbed her by the waist and dipped her into a kiss. She let him support her, enjoying the strength of his arms and shoulders. His nose and beard were cold against her face, but the kiss left her breathless.

Hazel steadied herself. "That was unexpected." Sam pointed up, and she followed his finger. The shop owner had hung mistletoe above the window.

CHAPTER

FOUR

"Oh, what a laugh, it would have been, if Daddy had only seen, Mommy kissing Santa Claus last night."

HAZEL AND ROSIE pulled into Amara's drive one after the other. It was serendipitous timing. They both knew the book club was about to be in on the knowledge of Rosie's pregnancy, and Rosie felt protective of the information. She'd expressed earlier that she was enjoying having their own little secret and wasn't ready to give it up yet.

Hazel offered a slew of suggestions, from skipping the meeting altogether to inventing any excuse for refusing a glass of wine; "Drank too much last weekend. Having a sober December. On the run from the NSA and have to remain sharp at all times." Still, Rosie had ultimately accepted that the thing to do was to let them know.

Somehow, even though Rosie regretted the need to tell them so soon, she was also excited to do so. "I don't know, Hazel; pregnancy is weird already."

They climbed the stairs to the porch, and Hazel asked, "Are you ready?"

Rosie gave a weak smile. "Let's do it."

They took the familiar path to the living room and were greeted by Amara and Lydia. Amara waved them to their usual places on the couch. "Tell us all about Hawaii!"

"We'll trade because I have to hear about Mumbai!" They discussed their recent travels, Rosie dwelling on the hiking and stunning views, Amara lamenting about her and Omar getting sick.

"We were having a great time until we weren't. The mix of new architecture and ancient all in one city was dizzying. Depending on where we were, it was like being in the future or the past! We got to see a beach if you could call it that. It didn't compare to what you described, for sure. Then we got terribly sick on the third day. I'll spare you the details." She looked at them darkly.

Jessica arrived while Hazel, Rosie, and Lydia commiserated with Amara. She slid into the room, stood directly before the coffee table, and took her jacket off with a flourish. She struck a super-hero pose, revealing her sweater, which read "Smut Slut" in large pink letters. Everyone howled, including Jessica, and she said, "I hope you ladies are ready." She plopped onto the cushioned chair next to Lydia.

Hazel interjected, "Wait, wait, I *have* to know where you got that shirt before we compare notes!"

"Hah! It came up in my Etsy feed. Isn't it perfect?"

"Beyond. Send me the link!"

Jessica sighed. "I missed this so much." Her eyes rolled back in her head. "I'm primed! Okay, *Santa's Huge Talent.* It's the holiday book of my wildest dreams. Is anyone else as jazzed as I am that it literally starts off with Mrs. Claus baking the dick shaped Christmas cookies? I almost died when she iced them."

Rosie nudged Hazel. "You went to the Gingerbread Competition. Any adult-shaped cookies there?"

"Sadly, no." The group feigned disappointment.

Amara picked up the conversation, "I did think those cookies were a clear sign of what to expect in the book. Then when it turned into the whole Goldielocks, which size is just right scene when Santa was there?"

Jessica nearly leapt to the end of her chair in excitement. "Yes! And he was all looking at the cookies, and she was being so coy, like, "Is this one the right size?" starting with the smallest one. And Santa was like, "Bigger, bigger, bigger.""

Lydia cleared her throat. "I think the idea of them being together for millennia and they're still into each other is sweet."

Jessica quipped, "In chapter two, the scene of them being into each other, literally, was pretty vivid." Lydia blushed and giggled.

Rosie asked, "Okay, I love all the sex, but can we also talk about the story? I wasn't really expecting there to be a mystery component. What's going on with the Christmas Magic? The elves eluded to helping raise it somehow, but they were worried about being able to."

Omar came in, balancing a tray of wine glasses. He knew each of their preferred wines by heart and acted the butler during their meetings, keeping the pours going. Hazel and Rosie shared a glance, and Hazel saw her take a long inhale.

Amara accepted her glass, then Hazel. As he held out a glass to Rosie, Jessica asserted, "I'm calling it right now. Christmas Magic is Sex Magic, and we're headed straight for an Elven Orgy." She slowed down the sentence as her eyes locked onto Rosie, politely declining the glass of white. The room was strangely quiet, and Omar's extended hand seemed to hang in the air.

Jessica broke the silence. "I'm just going to say what we're all thinking. There's no way you're knocked up. We know your man is fixed."

A huge smile spread across Rosie's face, but she kept her eyes on her knees. All attention was on her. "It's very rare, but sometimes the vas deferens can grow back together after a vasectomy."

Amara gasped. "Is this a happy accident, then?" Rosie nodded. The room erupted in cheers. Lydia pushed Hazel out of the way to claim a seat beside Rosie and hugged her, tears in the corner of her eyes.

Once the congratulations died down, Jessica added, "I guess this is the real Sex Magic. I've heard pregnancy sex is some of the absolute best, by the way."

"YOUR HOUSE IS my new favorite spot. Every time I come you've done up something new." Rosie gushed as she entered the kitchen. It was game night, and Munchkin Cthulhu was already set up. "Listen, what are you guys doing for New Year's Eve?" She sat down a paper grocery bag on the counter while Nick uncovered a veggie platter at the table.

Hazel eyed the bag wearily, "What's… uh… What's in there?"

Sam laughed. He had only recently learned about the true ongoings on Thanksgiving. "Feeling a little nervous, are you?"

Rosie lifted sparkling apple cider from the bag. "Don't worry, you no longer have to drink for two. I thought this would be fun for me while I'm banned. Though, I insist on drinking it from your fanciest glass." She winked at Hazel.

"Coming right up!" Hazel rifled through the small wet

bar area. "We haven't talked about New Year's plans yet. Sam, any ideas?"

"Not yet. Why do you ask?"

Nick appeared at his side holding a piece of broccoli. "You have plans now! BRD has rented a rooftop bar in Crestwood. They're putting on a masquerade. It's all anyone can talk about at work. Anyway, my boss owes me a favor, so I asked if I could have three plus ones, and he said yes."

Sam gave him a quizzical look, "Blue Ridge Designs… The same graphics company that does all the public health PSAs… is throwing a masquerade?"

"Oh yeah. They're real serious about it, too. Definitely a work hard, play hard situation."

Hazel poured sparkling cider straight to the top of a champagne flute. "We are definitely in! I remember the last time they did a party like this, and shit got downright silly. Didn't your CFO win the costume contest by showing up as a photographer, taking pictures of everyone all night, and then revealing it was him the whole time?"

"Yes! Plus, the pictures he captured are still used as blackmail today!"

The group moved toward the table, and Sam hummed in consideration. "Hazel, could you grab the Cowboy Munchkin deck too? I have a theory we could combine these and capture some real Mad Max vibes."

"Sure, okay." Hazel left to retrieve the game from their closet, and Sam hastily pulled out a black velvet box from his pocket.

"Just needed to get her outta here for a second; come here!"

Rosie waved her hands excitedly in the air as she sidled up to Sam. Nick came along his other side, and Sam opened the box. The rings within it were pristine and glimmered even in the low light. They were both white gold and the princess cut diamond, beautiful as it was, couldn't match the eye-catching quality of the other band.

"I've never seen anything like that before," Rosie whispered. It was both antique and current; the intricate leaf pattern was studded with tiny stones that barely hinted at their blue color. "She's going to love it."

"What are you guys doing?" Hazel had returned, Munchkin box in hand.

Rosie and Nick skirted around the table and took their chairs. Sam shoved the box back into his pocket. "This tomato looks exactly like a scary clown, but you have to see it in the right light. See?" Sam picked up a tomato from the platter and tilted it back and forth, pretending to examine it.

Hazel frowned after staring at the fruit for a minute. "Looks like a tomato to me."

Rosie snapped her fingers and pointed at her. "That's what I said!"

The night continued as it usually did on Munchkin nights. They all cheated (which is encouraged in the rules), and no one trusted anyone else to play a fair game. Each of them was called out for holding too many cards at once, and at one point, Sam was found to have equipped 5 hands' worth of gear when he only had two hands. Hazel smiled proudly, "I've taught you so well."

When Sam excused himself for the bathroom, Hazel whispered to her friends conspiratorially, "I'm planning a surprise for Sam."

Nick stumbled over his words, "You.. you are?"

Hazel could have sworn he and Rosie shared a glance, but she didn't have time to think about that. "His parents are coming Christmas week. It's the first time they'll visit us here. I can't believe I've set it all up, and he doesn't suspect a thing!"

The toilet flushed down the hall, and she backed away from leaning into the center table. "Okay, act normal." She hissed. This time Rosie definitely squinted her eyes at Nick. What were they up to?

CHAPTER

FIVE

" It's beginning to look a lot like Christmas, toys in every store. But the prettiest sight to see, is the holly that will be on your own front door."

HAZEL HAD DRIVEN into Crestwood alone to do some Christmas shopping but had largely struck out. She'd crawled the mall, hoping something would catch her eye. When nothing called to her there, she'd gone down the street to Target. This was slightly more successful. She at least left with ideas for Rosie and Nick; a set of fine knives and a butcher's block. On the drive back home, she made a last-minute decision to turn off at her old exit. The coffee shop she used to frequent was still open, so she picked up a latte, then made the short drive by her old home. The lights were on inside. Someone else had clearly rented the property. She parked on the street and watched the house for a minute, coffee warming her hands. It made her happy to know the house that had been so good to her was inhabited, and she hoped whoever was there was thriving and happy.

Although her intentions were deeply felt, it wasn't long before Hazel started to feel a bit of a creep, staring at a house she didn't live in. She rolled her eyes at herself and put the car back in drive. Not yet completely done with the impromptu tour, she continued past the house and into the historic district. Old, expensive houses lined both sides of the street here, each regally decorated for the season. This had been her favorite street to walk on for years, not because of the stately houses but because of the maple trees. No matter the season, they were stunning. The bright greens of Spring, deeper green hues of summer, and, best of all, the brightest yellows, oranges, reds, and pinks of fall. Even now, with all the foliage long since fallen, the light-colored bark and stretching branches were picturesque. Hazel crested a hill on the road and smiled as her favorite maple entered her view. "Hi Breezy, long time no see," she spoke to the tree as she drove past.

It wasn't until she was in bed, reading the last of *Santa's Huge Talent*, that an idea struck her. The perfect gift for Sam. She definitely wouldn't have found it in the mall or at Target. The thought made her snort. Sam side-eyed her, "Oh yeah?"

"You'll know when you get there. It's in chapter 19. I won't spoil you." He nodded and flipped a page of his copy.

TONIGHT WAS THE NIGHT. It was brutally cold out, but they were going to Hazel's all-time favorite holiday event, Winter Lights. Not only did she look forward to this night, maybe even more than Christmas itself, but there was no denying it was an enchanting atmosphere. The Botanical Gardens transformed into a fairy-like lighting experience where guests walked amongst millions of lights.

Sam checked and double-checked the lump in his pocket. He'd given a lot of thought to how the night could go and identified some basic steps for success. The main concern was the weather. By the end of the night, it would be below freezing. He'd dug through closets to find their warmest hats, scarves, jackets, gloves, and long johns. Reviewing the website led to another helpful discovery; he could preorder hot cocoa and s'mores kits, reducing time spent in line.

He strategically commented about the temperature going down throughout the day, and as Hazel dressed, Sam made sure she donned layers. He couldn't help getting caught up in her excitement as she anticipated the event. "What do you think will be different this year? They pretty much always have the big rainbow tree, but I'm expecting maybe a mushroom theme somewhere in the middle?"

"Mushrooms would be cool. I remember last year they had a forest of person-sized flowers that changed from orange to blue, green to white. That was spectacular."

"Ooh! Or the chandeliers from the trees! Those were a couple years ago; I'm not sure you were there for them." Hazel frowned slightly. "It feels like we've always been together. Then something like this happens, and I'm reminded you weren't there. You were off having your own experiences. Which, honestly, how dare you?"

Sam was driving, but Hazel's grin was visible even in his periphery. He scoffed. "Oh, I don't know, it sounds like you were also off admiring chandeliers without me! The nerve of some people." He shook his head and turned just enough to wink at her.

They pulled into the parking lot, and it was immediately apparent the freezing temperatures had not dissuaded the crowd. Sam found a spot in the back, and they trekked to the gardens' entry. The walk there also impressively alight. Large oak trees in the parking lot were each robed in their own twinkling hues. Pink, purple, blue, green, yellow, and white.

Hazel let out a thrilled squee as they stepped through the entry arch. The first section of the gardens was the simplest. Trees and shrubs were bedecked with light as if they were made of it. One large bush, in particular, was cloaked in bright white but had occasional bloom-like dots of yellow and orange that faded in and out.

Sam knew from last year that the rest of the display was in a long oval shape. The front middle held the most other-worldly arrangement. He planned to take the back path to the peak, where they would stop for cocoa and s'mores, then travel back down the front section. He would propose in the most beautiful spot there. However, taking this path was not as easy as it sounded because Hazel traveled by whim in the Winter Lights. She flitted from one exhibit that caught her eye to another. He overcame this by mirroring her behavior in the direction which suited his needs best. "Wow! Look at this one!" He would say, then scurry up the back path.

His plan was working brilliantly. They'd arrived toward the end and milled through the bonsai display toward the concessions. And not a moment too soon. Hazel's nose was distinctly red with cold. She was so beautiful and full of life. Sam stopped and watched her wind through the bonsais. It was frigid, but even covered with thick layers, and amongst many other onlookers, he could detect her energy. She spun as if she was caught in a whirlwind from the two kids skipping past her holding hands and then caught him staring. "What?"

"You're my favorite human, is all." She rolled her eyes, which amplified the green light reflecting off them.

"Stop staring, and come on. I'm turning into an icicle over here." Hazel chided him, blowing warm air onto her mittened hands.

Licking flames of campfires greeted them as they climbed the stairs and made the right turn to the north part of the event. Sam fished his phone out, explaining he had pre-purchased some things for them. "There, now you've got the confirmation on your phone. If you pick up the s'mores and start the roasting, I'll meet you with some cocoa.

Hazel dipped her chin and batted her eyes. "We are spoiled tonight! Getting both treats?"

Sam winked and replied, "I aim to please." He joined the fast-moving queue of people wielding phone screens with QR Codes indicating their purchase. Hazel did the same by the nearest fire. He couldn't hear her interaction with the attendant but her expression and the easy body language she assumed when she was relaxed made warmth grow in his chest. "Two cocoas with mint marshmallows, please." He presented his phone for scanning and was awarded two cups so hot he was glad to be wearing gloves.

By the time he joined Hazel, she was stabbing marshmallows onto the roasting sticks. She sighed in relief, "So glad you're back in time. I wasn't going to be able to bring myself to abuse your marshmallow the way you do."

"Abuse! You're still setting yours on fire, you know! I just like mine... well done."

"Burnt to a crisp, more like." She retorted and bumped his hip with hers.

Nerves Sam didn't expect began to kick in as they assembled and ate the s'mores. His gut squirmed uncomfortably. It wasn't as if he wasn't certain. He'd been sure for longer than he'd admit to most people. And he knew she would say yes. That was the relationship they had. So why the anxiety? Sam wasn't sure, but he couldn't bring himself to finish the s'more and stealthily discarded it.

They made their way down the front path, Sam trying to act natural but feeling overheated even in the chill night air. Fortunately, this part of the lights proved to be a show-stopper. Hazel buzzed about like a bee in a field of flowers in Spring. "They brought back the chandeliers! There! They're a little different this time, but so cool!" She grabbed his hand and tugged him until they were directly beneath dimly lit and ornate purple and blue chandeliers. They were haunting. Should he do it here? His stomach lurched, and he decided to wait. He would know when they reached the perfect spot.

Further along the trail, they entered what could only be described as a fairytale. Hazel stopped dead and squealed, "There ARE mushrooms!" Spotted mushrooms sized from realistically small to so large they could easily be sat on were scattered through the landscape amongst trees and delicate paper flowers lit from within. On one side, artistic interpretations of grass swaying with light-made butterflies which appeared to flitter along a path. Along the trail ahead was an arched footbridge, and even the water running beneath it was lit. This was the place! The bridge in this garden that made magic seem real was the perfect spot.

Sam's mouth was dry as he took the first step onto the short but wide bridge. In another four, they were in the center. He stopped and stared down into the water. The lights were at the bottom of the stream, and the gentle water ripples gave the impression of liquid metal.

"Hazel?"

"Mmm." She answered but didn't look up from the mesmerizing water.

Sam swallowed and reached into his pocket to touch the box there. "I have something important to ask you." Hazel moved her eyes to him, smiling brightly as any of the displays.

The crowd of people around them started clapping and cheering. For one confused moment, Sam thought they somehow knew he was about to propose. Then Hazel joined, clapping and shouting a protracted "Woohoo!" Sam followed her gaze and found another man on the other side of the bridge, unmistakably mid-proposal. He was on one knee, holding a small open box in front of a woman, her mouth open in surprise. He didn't hear her response through the crowd, but she must have said yes because she pulled up the man and kissed him, garnering even more applause.

Sam withdrew his hand from his pocket as the flow of people resumed a regular walking pattern. Hazel skipped to his side and wrapped an arm around his waist. "What were you going to ask?"

"Huh?"

"You said you had something important to ask me about?"

Sam tried to fight the daze settling upon him at what had just occurred. "Ah, I was thinking about the masquerade. If we want good costumes, we should start shopping now. New Years is coming fast."

Hazel waggled her finger in the air. "I'm so glad you brought this up because I have opinions!" They walked back to the car together, dreaming up mask themes. Sam was not fully engaged as he mentally regrouped his proposal plans. Maybe there was something to be said about wrapping the ring and putting it at the bottom of her stocking. It'd be a private event. She wouldn't expect something like that to be in a stocking and wouldn't find it until everything else was unwrapped and nothing could possibly get in the way.

Hazel obsessively checked the time but tried to do it in a way that wasn't too obvious. She made excuses to walk through the kitchen to see the digital display on the oven or pass the bookshelf in the living room with a clock on it. Sam's parents had flown out early in the morning. It would be a big surprise for him no matter when they arrived, yet she was hopeful they'd walk through the door at dinner time. It was a possibility as long as there were no significant flight delays.

Don and Summer, Sam's father and stepmother, were a close-knit group. They were also the only resistance Hazel felt when Sam decided to move to Crestwood. She understood, and in the end, they were supportive. Still, she worried they secretly harbored a little resentment toward her. It wasn't as if they were overtly rude; the contrary! Everyone had a lovely time when they visited Portland, and they always included Hazel on their weekly FaceTime calls. She still felt pressure to make this trip a great one for them. It was their first time coming to Crestwood, and she wanted them to love it.

The trouble started around 4:30pm. Their plane should have landed, and Hazel was watching her phone for messages from Summer to confirm. Since she couldn't pick them up, the plan was to order them an Uber. Hazel kept herself busy by prepping the spinach lasagna they'd eat for dinner. She was stirring the egg, cottage cheese, and herb mixture when Sam swept into the kitchen, hugged her from behind, and asked where he could jump in. Hazel could not recall a time she wanted his help less but struggled to find a way to shake him.

"I've got this on lock. Why don't you relax and play the new Zelda?"

Sam was already grabbing down two wine glasses. "I'd much rather make dinner with this pretty lady I know." He turned his head toward the small white speaker on the far counter. "Hey Siri, play 90's hip-hop." He balanced a full glass in each hand, waving them gently above his head as he ground against Hazel's backside.

Hazel couldn't help but laugh. She turned to face him, straddled his thigh, shimmied her shoulders, and reached up to relieve a glass from him. When she turned back toward the counter, her phone screen turned off. "Can you wilt the spinach? I need to use the bathroom." She swiped her phone off the counter as she left.

SUMMER PIERCE

> We don't see you anywhere, sweetie, are you here? 4:35pm

HAZEL SLUMPED, crestfallen. They'd talked about the plans ad nauseam! Would they be disappointed now?

Hazel

> Hey Sumer! I hope your flight was uneventful. I'm going to order you an Uber, remember? Now I know you're here I'm on it! 4:36pm

HAZEL OPENED the Uber App as fast as possible and ordered a car to pick them up. When she opened her Messages again, she saw that Summer was typing back to her, but she didn't wait for the reply.

> Just got confirmation that Aaron will be
> there to pick you up in 10 minutes! He's
> driving a white Honda Civic. Looks like this-
> 4:39pm

SHE ATTACHED an image of the reservation screen.

SUMMER PIERCE

> That's right. We've never done the uber
> before. Thank you. See you soon. 4:41pm

HAZEL LET OUT A SLOW EXHALE. That wasn't so bad. Plus, the timing seemed to be working out.

Hazel waited on tenterhooks for the doorbell, her eyes still flitting to the clock as she counted down their arrival. She and Sam were sitting at the table about to dig into their meal when it rang. Sam looked up curiously, "Package?" Hazel shrugged. When it rang again, he got up from his seat. "Are Nick and Rosie coming over?"

"I don't think so," Hazel replied, rising from her seat but purposefully staying behind Sam with her camera ready.

As Sam opened the door, she watched through the camera as she snapped a flurry of photos. Don and Summer didn't hesitate to come inside and nearly shouted Sam's name in greeting. Sam was stunned but quickly swept his Dad, then Summer, into a hug. Then turned his eyes upon Hazel, who was still documenting the event.

"You did this?" He asked.

"Merry Christmas! We have them for the holiday."

Hazel ushered them to the table while Sam grabbed their luggage.

THE SURPRISE ARRIVAL of his parents was a fantastic gift. Sam couldn't wait to show them the sights and their new home and spend time with them. At the same time, he was getting frustrated with his proposal plans being thwarted. Even as they first stepped into his home, Sam realized proposing with them here didn't feel right, and he'd have to reconsider the plan yet again.

CHAPTER
SIX

"Sleigh bells ring, are you listening? In the lane, snow is glistening. A beautiful sight, we're happy tonight. Walking in a winter wonderland."

CHRISTMAS WAS FOUR DAYS AWAY. Sam's parents would be with them until they took their early morning flight back to Portland the day after the holiday. By the evening of the first full day with their guests, Sam noted it might be best to have them stay in a local hotel or B&B next time.

They were great. Talkative. Lively. Funny. Kind… Exhausting. It was like they didn't have an off button. So much so it led to some awkward interactions that Don and Summer were oblivious about.

During the day, Sam and Hazel were at work. Well, they tried to work. Summer didn't seem to understand that working from home required as much concentration and effort as working in an office and kept interrupting them. Sam was meeting with several marketing executives at noon when Summer opened his office door and loudly announced she'd made lunch. Sam swiftly turned his camera off and mouthed, "Not now," until she retreated. The lesson didn't stick, however, because she did the same thing to Hazel minutes later. Once they got a chance to surface for lunch, Sam asked her not to enter their offices unannounced. Summer interpreted this as a request for her to knock loudly on their doors, and when that didn't work, the text messaging began.

After work, they decided to go to Pico, a trendy fusion restaurant in downtown Crestwood. The menu was a foodie dreamscape that changed frequently based on what was in season. It was known as one of the gems of Crestwood and was often featured in media as being the height of Caribbean Mexican cuisine. This, however, did not land with Don. Sam secretly felt Don was being purposefully difficult when he insisted he couldn't understand the menu enough to make an order, but couldn't imagine why he would want to do that. After 10 minutes of baffled sounds and gestures towards the small menu in his hands, Don asked Summer to order for him.

Dinner was lovely after orders were made. Summer was so outgoing she was conducting conversations with the tables on both sides of them. The table to the left was an older couple who was flying down to Florida to be with their kids for the holiday; they discussed packing and travel woes and recommended the beaches in Florida as a must-see. To the right was a group of three friends out celebrating a career change. One of the women had accepted a role as a receptionist for a local law firm, and it would enable her to work regular business hours. Summer praised the 9 to 5 workday, saying, "Oh, you can have a family dinner now!" Sam bristled slightly at the assumption and saw Hazel stiffen across the table from him, but the conversation continued to flow.

A different waiter delivered their check at the end of the night. He spoke with a slight accent, "No rush here.

Please take your time and enjoy. This is here when you're ready." He slipped the black folder next to Sam, who had raised his hand to receive it.

Don cocked his head to the side at the waiter. "Your accent. Are you from here?"

Hazel's eyes popped.

The waiter stood silent for a moment, then carefully replied, "I, um, grew up in LA."

Summer waved her hand dismissively. "He means your heritage! Your parents moved here from somewhere?"

"Mom!" Sam exhaled the exclamation under his breath.

"What? We're curious!" She looked around, baffled, but finding no support, continued, "Oh! I'm sorry. We aren't racist or anything. I'm glad we're a melting pot, you know!"

Sam put his credit card into the folder and handed it to the waiter, who seemed relieved to have an excuse to exit. Sam said sternly, "You can't ask people things like that. He was probably horrified you were going to say something disgusting next."

Don shook his head, "Well then, how do you ask?"

"You don't! Not with strangers. Why would it matter?"

Don dismissed Sam. "We're just showing a personal interest."

"You could have asked him anything, though. Where he got his hat, about the earring he was wearing, his favorite menu item."

As Sam and Hazel got ready for bed, they compared notes from the evening. Hazel spit her toothpaste into the sink. "That was the wildest dinner I've ever had. What were they thinking?"

Sam took a turn spitting his toothpaste out. "Portland… is not very racially diverse. I think they just have no clue how that question probably hit the guy.”

Hazel raised an eyebrow but moved on, “And Summer! The biggest social butterfly I have ever seen. Ever.”

Sam chuckled. “She’s always been like that. She can talk to anyone and will do it as long as you let her.”

“I was honestly impressed. Kinda cool to get to know a little about your restaurant neighbors.” Hazel lay in their bed. “I am tired from all the socializing, though.”

“How’s the visit going, Hazel? Sam’s folks are in town, right?” Lydia sat crosslegged on the loveseat, holding her glass of rosé. The book club had thoroughly dissected the ending of *Santa’s Huge Talent* and were catching up.

Hazel paused before replying. Exactly long enough for Jessica to let out a low whistle and ask, “That good, huh?”

Hazel put her hands up as if pushing against the reaction. “No, it’s not been bad at all. They are sweet, and we’ve had a great time so far. It’s just different having them here all the time, and I keep wondering if they’re enjoying themselves, you know?”

Rosie and Amara replied simultaneously. Rosie smacked her knee and said, “Of course, they’re having a good time.” Amara asked, “What makes you doubtful?”

Hazel shrugged. “Little things. We went to Pico, and Don had issues with the menu. We took them hiking, something I know they do, but Summer kept commenting on the unkempt trail. Then we ate at home last night, and they know I’m a pescatarian; we served butternut tacos. Not spicy because I know they like it mild, and they asked where the protein was. I was like, “In the beans?” She gestured toward invisible beans.

Jessica exclaimed, “Hah! Right in the beans! That’s

what the lead elf should have said during the nude snow-ball fight." They chuckled, recalling the scene before she continued more seriously. "Being real, it sounds like those are minor things and equate to differences for them. They'll probably have their own version of this conversation when they're back home."

Rosie nodded forcefully. "Exactly! They'll explain to their friends that they had a great time and you were wonderful, but sharing a bathroom with other adults was weird or something. There's always little oddities traveling and sharing space, but it doesn't mean they aren't having fun."

"Thanks, ladies. I can always count on you to talk me off a ledge," Hazel smirked, "Now let me tell you all my worries about the gifts."

Everyone laughed, and the conversation moved on, but Hazel was serious. When she was wrapping them, it occurred to her that Sam could not possibly open his main presents in front of his parents. She'd already been self-conscious about her gifts for them. They had to fit in suit-cases and be allowed on flights which were limiting factors. Now Sam would also exclusively be unwrapping small items in front of them. Sam might also think it was weird, but she'd make it up to him later; his parents would think she was cheap or a lousy gifter. Considering Christmas Eve was tomorrow, there wasn't much to do to rectify anything.

To Hazel's delight, Christmas Eve was going swimmingly. They'd decided to make a traditional family dinner that night and began prepping after lunchtime. Sam had purchased a ham for Don and Summer. Over breakfast, they jokingly told them they'd need to make it, only to discover they absolutely wanted to.

Hazel felt as if she was getting to peek into a window to

Sam's past as they all worked in the kitchen, whirling around each other. Hazel made a winter greens salad with apple and lemony vinaigrette and helped Sam chop more apples for the pie while he worked the dough. Don reduced a pineapple glaze for the ham that looked so incredible Hazel asked if she could use it on top of her rustic carrot and farro dish. Summer zipped around amongst them, helping where she could, keeping the kitchen clean, and leading them in song when one of her preferred holiday pieces started playing in the background.

Hazel and Sam were cleaning dishes after their delicious meal when the doorbell rang. From the living room, they heard Don question, "People are delivering this late on Christmas Eve?!"

Sam replied, "Not exactly." While Hazel answered the door. She waved to Nick, who was already backing his car out of the drive.

"I'll be right back!" Hazel called as she let the front door close behind her. She returned in 5 minutes and shouted into the house, "All set!"

She could hear Sam and his parent's voices get nearer as they approached. He helped open the door for them, saying, "I think you're really going to love this." Hazel stood in the yard in the center of four bicycles, each wrapped in string lights.

Summer took in the sight and asked, "What is this?"

Hazel explained, "This is something my parents and I used to do every Christmas Eve. Decorate our bikes and ride around the neighborhood to enjoy all the houses one last time. Rosie and Nick let us borrow their bikes so we could all go."

"Isn't that wonderful!" Summer sounded like she really meant it. Though she was Sam's stepmother, at the moment, her bright smile reminded Hazel of Sam's. They fetched their coats, donned helmets, and took off.

Hazel knew this was the highlight of the trip 10 minutes in when Summer and Don spread their legs wide and let gravity take them down a hill, cheering like children. They ranked their favorite houses, playfully arguing about which they preferred. Don had a proclivity for yards with inflatables which put his ranking at odds with everyone else. Summer picked the exact opposite style; classic white lights and evergreen wreaths. Hazel wondered how they decorated their own house, considering.

They were in a particularly festive cul de sac, admiring four homes that were clearly competing for best dressed Hazel pointed toward one with rainbow lights around the trim, over their bushes, and wrapping around the bases of all their trees. "They win for sure. It might as well be a doll house."

Summer disagreed. "Too much color, it makes it messy. This one isn't the best we've seen, but it's the best one here." She indicated a home with white lights around the front windows and entry.

Don mimed, pulling his hair out above his helmet. "You're all crazy! How can you not like the whimsy of the inflatable Santa sleigh on their roof? Santa is on their roof! It's canon!"

Sam bit back a smirk, eyes glinting with cheer. "I love all of this." He made circles before him with his hands.

Hazel asked, "We were going to turn around and head back here, but there's one more house we can't miss if you're up for it? It's probably two blocks away." Everyone eagerly agreed to keep going, so she led the way.

There were fewer decorated houses in this area, so they made quick time. Hazel saw the faint glow of the house she was leading them toward before they even turned onto its street. After they made the right, she sped up to reach it, then stopped before the spectacle. Don gapped at the house. "Oh my…"

There were no less than 70 inflatables. So many that although they tried to count, they never agreed on the same number. Small, simple candy canes were next to enormous snow globes with rotating carousels inside. Numerous snowmen, elves, reindeer, Santa and Mrs. Claus, abominable snowmen, dragons, gingerbread cookies, gift boxes, Snoopy, and many other characters. The longer they observed, the more they saw.

Don excitedly pointed out everything he noticed. His pure enthusiasm brought joy to all of them. After five full minutes of exclaimed discoveries, he turned to Hazel. "Thank you for this. Thank you so much." He grabbed her into a firm hug. Hazel couldn't be sure, but she thought his eyes were shining a bit silvery.

Sam mixed hot cocoa for them to warm up when they returned home. As they drank in the living room, Summer reflected, "You know, I think we'll need to make this our tradition on Christmas Eve too. Thanks for sharing this with us, Hazel. I think I can speak for all of us. We treasured this."

Hazel's throat constricted while her heart seemed to expand. She shook her head at her feet, trying to control her tear ducts, which were betraying her. "You don't know how much it means for me to share something my family did with you."

There was silence for a beat before Summer cleared her throat. "I know… it's not anywhere near the same, but you're part of our family now."

There was no holding back the tear that trickled from Hazel's eye then. She let it fall. Summer embraced her while Sam placed a hand on her knee.

CHAPTER
SEVEN

"The mood is right, the spirits up. We're here tonight and that's enough. Simply having a wonderful Christmas time."

THE SLANTING Christmas morning light filtered through the window, gold and glorious. Hazel lay in their bed watching it. She was perfectly comfortable wrapped in her blanket. The house was silent. She was excited for the day to come but knew the moment she put foot to floor, it would be celebration. So she drank in the quiet and peace for a few minutes.

Sam's breathing changed behind her, and Hazel smiled. "Merry Christmas."

Sam sleepily breathed, "Merry Christmas to you."

The wood was cold beneath her feet, so Hazel hastened to her closet to don her favorite slippers. After brushing her teeth and running a brush through her hair, she started coffee brewing in the kitchen. As it steeped, she leaned against the entry to the living room, enjoying the Christmas tree. The lights still danced amongst the branches. Gifts were piled beneath, and the stockings were magically much fuller than the night before.

Craving a sweet treat, Hazel investigated her stocking. She'd just reached in when she heard Sam's reprimand, "Nah uh, uh. You can't get started without me!"

Hazel spun around, her hair whipping behind her. "Just a little chocolate nibble."

"So presumptive! How do you know there's chocolate in there?" Sam moved to her as he spoke and started dancing with her. "I've got something sweet for you." He kissed her temple.

"I don't see any mistletoe over there." Don appeared out of the hallway, followed by Summer.

Summer outpaced him and gathered Sam and Hazel into a hug, crooning, "Oh! Merry Christmas, everyone!"

They prepared coffee in the kitchen, then relocated into the living room for gift opening. Hazel sat next to the base of the tree and passed a box to each person. Sam kept trying to get Hazel to open her own gifts at the same time, but this was a surprising challenge for her. She wanted to watch everyone else and talk to them; her instinct was to keep their hands full. This resulted in Hazel having a pile of unopened presents after everyone else had unwrapped theirs.

Feeling in the spotlight, Hazel received a luxurious silk kimono hand painted with cherry blossoms, a mushroom lamp that glowed different colors when you booped the top of it, a print of one of her favorite fae book characters from *A Clan of Fog and Destiny*, and solar powered flower stakes for the yard to line their walkway. All from Sam, all so thoughtful. She felt moved and a little guilty. He'd only opened a few small gifts from her; a Flip Belt which promised to be an excellent solution for carrying phones while running, a hot sauce subscription box that would bring them flavors throughout the year, and two pairs of joke knee-high socks that made the wearer look like they had chicken legs.

It could have been worse. Don and Summer at least had loved their gifts. Sam secretly took delivery the day before of some specially ordered jelly donuts from a local place they adored, Ashbor-dough. Another surprise hit was the adult coloring books and pencil sets. Summer was so excited about them she started her first page while they enjoyed the donuts.

Hazel immediately tried on her new robe after breakfast. The fabric was so lustrous against her skin it was like being wrapped in cool air. "Think I could wear this to meetings? It's too comfortable; I don't want to take it off. Ever." Sam laughed, those perfect teeth flashing, and she had the urge to tell him… She could tell him right then, whisper in his ear, that he had more gifts coming, but they had to wait until tomorrow. Hazel grounded herself instead and resisted. If she told him now, he would know the nature of the surprise, and she wouldn't rob him of that.

Sam, Don, and Summer made a holiday mimosa in the kitchen. Remembering the promise of chocolate in her stocking, Hazel slipped back out to it. She brought the whole thing back to the kitchen table and dumped it. To her surprise, there was something wrapped at the bottom. She picked up the small envelope and turned it over. "What's this?"

Sam appeared next to her with her mimosa. "I don't know. Guess you better open it."

Hazel slid her finger beneath the envelope flap and pulled out a card. The invitation to the masquerade ball on New Year's Eve. The front was black with a silver mask and the information for the event etched beneath. It was a beautiful card, but she already knew all this. She flipped it over and recognized Rosie's handwriting. *We'd like to stop by tonight around 6pm. Sam said it was okay. See you soon.* What were they up to? True, they didn't usually see each other on Christmas, but of course, they could. She narrowed her eyes at Sam, "Do you know why?"

Sam shook his head. "I swear I don't. They asked if they could stop by but wouldn't say anything else."

Rosie and Nick arrived at 5:58pm; Hazel knew because she was counting the minutes. After opening the envelope, she shot Rosie a text probing for information, was shut down completely, and told to wait.

Polite introductions were made between Sam's parents and their friends. Don and Summer recognized their names from conversation and remembered it was their bikes they had borrowed yesterday and thanked them soundly.

The group settled into the living room, chatting cheerfully. "Since you're here, you can open these now! They go together. One sec." Hazel pulled a large, heavy package from the back of the tree. She strained to pick it up, hobbled over to Nick, and set it at his feet. "That's over your weight limit." She nodded toward Rosie, returned to the tree to fetch a medium box that was obviously lighter, and passed it to Rosie.

Nick leaned over the heavy box and picked it up to place on his lap, exclaiming, "Good grief! What is in here?" Hazel rolled her eyes to the left and waited for them to rip into the paper.

Rosie's package held the set of Henckels kitchen knives that came in a specialty block which honed each blade as it was pulled out. It was easy to understand, and all of them oohed and aahed. When Nick unwrapped the butcher's block, he understood what it was right away, but Don and Summer shared perplexed expressions with each other at his excitement. Summer asked, "Is it like a giant cutting board?"

Nick gleefully replied. "Yes, but mostly no. It's like the best cutting board in the world. One that's heavy enough to never slide around, large enough to prepare anything at all, they're made of all end grain which means they'll never get cut or scarred up. This one even has a channel around it," he flipped the top to face them and pointed to the shallowed rim, "we can push scraps or liquid into there for easy cleanup." He turned to face Hazel and Sam, "These are so good! Thank you so much! It's official. We're hosting dinner next."

Rosie sniffed and looked at the corner of the couch. She wasn't easily emotional, and Hazel wasn't sure what the best response was. "Are you okay?"

"Anytime you ask that, it only makes it worse." Rosie cried and laughed at once. "My hormones are off the rails, and I cry at anything! And now…" She was sobbing worse and worse and becoming hard to understand. "Now you're the only people who gave us gifts unrelated to the baby! And I just love you so much!"

Hazel swept across the room to her in a flash. "People really gave you presents for the baby? Isn't that for the baby shower?"

Rosie waved the question off, "We are so grateful for everything. I'm not complaining, I swear! I didn't even realize until we opened these. Something about being recognized as the people we still are now hit me in the feels." Her tears had settled, and Hazel began to say something in reply, but Rosie gasped, "Wait. There's more." Hazel sat back on the couch. Rosie swallowed hard and shared a look with Nick.

"Do you want me to?" Nick asked gently. Rosie shook her head and swallowed again.

"I can do it." She closed her eyes, reopened them, and

focused directly on Hazel. "We would be honored," Her voice shook, "if you would be the godparents."

Hazel put her hands over her mouth. She looked at Sam, then back at Rosie, then at Nick, who nodded encouragingly, then back to Rosie. Tears welled in her eyes, and she found her own voice wobbly. "Are you fucking kidding me?! I would be honored! I am honored! Oh my god." She wrapped her arms around Rosie.

Nick said, "This goes for you too, mate."

Sam was still sitting across the room from them. He pointed to himself, "Me?"

"Yes, you!"

Sam leapt in the air with a loud "whoop!" and came to hug Nick.

"We're godparents!" Hazel exclaimed at Sam, who was beaming so much his other cheek also dimpled. "This is the best Christmas ever."

CHAPTER
EIGHT

"Come and trim my Christmas tree, with some decorations bought at Tiffany. I really do believe in you, let's see if you believe in me."

SAM NEEDN'T HAVE SET his alarm for 4:45am because his parent's alarm began sounding at 4:15am and woke him up all the same. It was a mystery why they would rise so early and how Hazel remained peacefully resting. Her hair was partly covering her face and moved slightly at every exhale. What if he slid on her engagement ring while she was sleeping, and she would simply wake up with it on? Instead, he rolled out of bed, brushed his teeth, and started the coffee.

Summer spoke behind him as Sam pressed the button to grind the coffee beans, causing him to jump and let go of it. "Why are you up so early?" Then, "Oh, sorry." When he startled.

He pressed the button again and raised his eyebrows, "Heard your alarm go off. Why are *you* up so early?"

"I wanted to take a shower before we head out."

"We aren't leaving until 5:30; how long are you going to be in there?" Sam teased.

Summer shooed him with her hand, "I don't have time for your judgment." She winked before turning on her heel. Sam heard the bathroom door close, and the water pipes activated soon after. He scrolled through the news on his phone until the coffee was ready to pour, made two cups, then balanced them into the bedroom.

Hazel was still fast asleep. He carefully set her mug on the nightstand beside book one of the *Hazenative* trilogy, which they'd begun to read together. She stirred and, without so much as cracking an eye, mumbled, "I smell something… wonderful."

"Your sixth sense about the nearness of coffee is a true marvel of our times."

She groaned and stretched. "What do I need to do to wake up to the sweet, warm smell of coffee every day?" Her face turned suddenly serious. "Except not this early. What time is it? It's still all dark!"

Sam nodded, an exaggerated frown on his face, "It's 4:30. Mom apparently requires the world's longest shower before flying. I think she may be overestimating the capabilities of our water heater."

Hazel sat up and took a sip from her cup, closing her eyes again and focusing on the warm liquid flowing through her body. "Thank you for the delivery."

Saying goodbye to his parents was emotionally complicated. Sam didn't have a lot of experience with it. He'd lived with them as a child and in the same city as an adult until moving last year. Despite his expertise in communication and love of working remotely, FaceTime videos were not the same as having dinner together at the drop of a hat. He tried to put all the feelings coursing through him into each hug as they parted at the airport. Sam's stomach somersaulted when he saw how Hazel also embraced them. A little extra firm. A little longer than usual.

THE SHORT CAR ride back home was quiet. At first, Sam thought Hazel was likely just tired; however, when they were stopped at a light, he saw she was wide awake and had her thinking hard face on. "Whatcha thinking about?" She giggled. Was she nervous?

Her answer, "Nothing in particular," was a most obvious lie. She failed to hide the roguish smile that overtook her expression, and her face turned a bright fuchsia. She was most definitely up to something, but Sam couldn't think of anything that would make her react this way. It was almost like he'd caught her in the act of something embarrassing.

Sam plopped onto the couch. "Tomorrow is back to work. What should we do with the rest of the day?"

Hazel stood before him and was playing with his hand. "I want to give you a fashion show. I haven't tried on some of the new stuff from Christmas."

He sat upright. "I love a fashion show when you're the model. Strut it out, lady!"

Hazel giggled, dropping his hand. "Okay! You stay here!" She ran down the hall and closed the bedroom door behind her.

It took quite a bit of time for her to get ready. Sam glanced around the room, still a little messy from Christmas, and spotted the chicken leg socks. If Hazel was giving him a fashion show, he should give her one too! He rolled up the grey sweatpants he had on and pulled on the knee-high socks. Sam couldn't help but laugh out loud. The black background of the socks behind the thin orange chicken leg did give a hilarious effect. He positioned himself on the couch in a side-lying seductive pose and waited.

Hazel walked down the hall toward him slowly. He immediately knew what she was wearing wasn't anything that had been gifted to her. It was a sparkling black floor-length gown with sheer panels overlaying the solid fabric. It clung to her every curve effortlessly as if it had been hand-stitched for her. High slits on each side of the bottom showed glimpses of her thighs with each step. The top was gathered in a delicate halter around her neck. Her hair was styled so it was pinned back but was purposefully messy and textured. She was wearing prosthetic elf ears.

Hazel bit her lip as she entered the room, and Sam sat upright, abandoning his would-be pose and giving her his full attention. His sweatpants fell over the socks. "You look…" he started, but Hazel raised a finger to her lips and gestured for him to follow. Her hips swayed enticingly on the way back to the bedroom. But the bedroom… Several things caught Sam's eye at once. There was a tray on the bed with an assortment of candy canes and bottles of something along the side that might be lotions. Even curiouser, something hung from the ceiling. It had black metal at the top and some straps with padding dangled from it. When had that eye hook been installed in the ceiling? Sam nearly asked but then recalled he had been shushed before and kept silent. He may not be entirely sure what was happening, but his erection was ready for whatever came.

Sam tore his eyes from the black hanging contraption and put them back on Hazel, who was adjusting the candy canes on the tray. She picked the smallest one up and said, "I've been wondering which of these is the right size for you." Memories of *Santa's Huge Talent* flashed through his mind.

"I think that one might be a little small." His voice came out several pitches lower than usual.

Hazel picked up the next candy cane. "How about this one?" She giggled but quickly recovered her serious demeanor.

Sam shook his head. "We're going to need one… much bigger. If you need to, you could touch and then try again." She looked over her shoulder at him, mischief in her eyes, then approached. Hazel ran her hand up the inside of his thigh slowly and cupped his cock.

"Mmm. You're right." She let her other hand join the exploration. His dick was making a tent out of his sweats, and throbbed as she grasped him. "Thick, too. Yes, we need a much bigger cane." She turned back to the tray. It was everything Sam could do not to pounce her. He knew her sticking her backside out toward him was part of the plan, but damn. Damn. "How about this?" She turned around with the largest candy cane he'd ever seen. It wasn't made out of the usual ingredients but was some sort of twisted dough. She started deep-throating the candy cane. He watched it disappear into her mouth almost completely and couldn't stand it anymore.

"That's it. The perfect size. Maybe you could do that to me?"

Hazel took his t-shirt off first and ran her hands down his abdomen. She reached up to him and kissed him passionately. Sam could feel her breasts against his chest. Her hands were teasing around the waistband of his sweatpants. She pulled away from the kiss, hooked two fingers under his pants and briefs, and lowered them and her body to the floor. Sam closed his eyes as he felt his dick freed from the clothing.

Hazel wheezed with laughter. Sam, confused, opened his eyes and was reminded he was still wearing the chicken socks. He barreled over, laughing with her. "Oh, my God!"

Hazel said between fits. "I was not expecting that. They are so… so funny! I'm so sorry." She tried to get back into character.

"No, you're right. They're hilarious! I forgot I put them on! Let me just…" Sam peeled the socks off and tossed them to the side.

Hazel hummed deeply. "Much better. Now where was I?" Her eyes lit on his cock. "That's right…" She resumed kneeling before him and performed the same engulfing motion she'd done on the candy cane. Sam could feel the back of her throat against the head of his penis, and his whole body shuddered. The way she swirled her tongue around him every time she pulled away, drove him mad. Sam mentally tried to ignore the sensation so he wouldn't explode right then and there. His head tilted back in delight. Sam reached down to her and brushed Hazel's hair out of her eyes. She looked up at him and maintained eye contact as she pushed his cock deeper into her mouth. That was enough.

"Should I… Mmm… Call you Mrs. Claus?" Sam was on the edge and finding it difficult to make complete sentences. Hazel pulled back with a flicker of her tongue on his frenulum.

She purred, "Call me whatever you like."

"I'll call you water then because I need a drink." Sam kneeled down and picked Hazel up from the floor, tossing her gently onto the bed. He flipped up her dress, grabbed her under the knees, and dragged her to the bed's edge. Sam slowly licked up her center, teasing her labia with his tongue, then growled, "It's so hot to find you wet after you've gone down on me." Hazel gasped as he dove into her. Sam ran his tongue circularly across every crease, flicking and sucking, Hazel squirming beneath him. When he reached her clitoris, he slowed and enjoyed the moan that escaped her lips as he took her in. He kept a slow pace, pulsing over her clit, then started fingering her with the same rhythm. Sam reached deep within her with two fingers pressing up and back. He quickened his movements adding swirls around her clit until Hazel's hips bucked with him.

"Stop, stop, stop." Hazel's command was barely audible, but he pulled back obediently. She stood up, walked to his other side, and pushed him on the bed.

Hazel grabbed one of the bottles and unscrewed the lid. "I've got some things for us to play with." She lifted the lid to reveal a puffy brush. "This is body powder; it should taste like raspberries." She dipped the brush into the powder and used it along his shoulders and chest. It was feathery and ticklish like Sam imagined putting on makeup would be. She reached for another bottle. "Now I'm going to paint you." She took turns using yellow, blue, and orange paints, half massaging them onto his chest, abs, arms, and even a stripe across his forehead. The sensation was not unpleasant, though he couldn't decipher if she made any sort of design. Hazel got up from the bed, and Sam protested. "If you get to decorate me like a cupcake, surely I get to do you!?" She smirked and rifled through the drawer of her nightstand. In a flash, the light changed, and Sam could see the paint was blacklight reactive. His torso was glowing with color.

"You're going to paint me… by using what's on you." Sam bit his lip, letting her plan sink in.

"Yes, except one thing." He stood behind her and slowly unzipped her dress and let it fall around her feet. He used the brush to apply the powder from her shoulders to her breasts. Even it shimmered slightly in the light. Then he opened the blue paint, the least reactive and hardest to decipher of the colors, dipped a finger in, and wrote, "Mrs. P" across her abdomen.

Hazel giggled as the cool paint tickled her. "What'd you put?"

Sam smiled. He let his fingers linger on her soft skin, enjoying the lines of her body. "That's for me to know and you to find out." He swooped her onto the bed, and they held each other as they fell into the sheets. Sam grabbed his cock and gently pushed into her, closing his eyes to savor the pleasure of their connection at last. Hazel wrapped her legs around his back, and Sam responded by thrusting into her, swiveling his hips. He saw her chest flush and kissed her neck. "It *does* take like raspberries!" He ran the back of his tongue down her chest, then sucked at her nipple. The feeling of the paint between them was novel. It was like a slick gel, and it assumed their body temperature.

Hazel licked him neck to ear, then lightly nipped his ear lobe with her teeth. She breathed into his ear, and Sam felt shivers down his back. She kissed him, their tongues twisting around each other.

Sam reared into an upright position and lifted Hazel's hips. She moaned in reply, but it was cut short, turning into a whimper when he drove into her. Her eyes popped open, and the heat in her chest raised. He could feel her inner muscles contract around him. Sam slowed down and leaned forward again to kiss her.

Hazel exhaled, "I think we're ready to try the swing." She nodded toward the hanging straps.

Sam's mouth fell into an O. "The swing!?" She grinned deviously and looked at him through the top of her eyes.

"The swing," Hazel confirmed. She rolled out from under him and separated the straps. "I've never done this before, but I think this one is where you sit, then the other one kinda holds your low back, and these two are the stirrups." She used the corner of the bed to climb into the swing. Sam stood before her and helped position her feet into the stirrups. The result was a floating Hazel, feet spread wide, gloriously open, and a mess of paint glowing all over her body.

Sam didn't need further instruction. He positioned himself in front of her, guided his cock into her once again, then grabbed hold of the metal bar the straps dangled from. It was a sensation he'd never experienced before. Like gravity was different. The usual restraints on movement were no longer. Hazel's whole body moved with the lightest touches; her breast bounced with every thrust. "You are a shining goddess. Literally, floating."

Hazel wrapped her legs around his back, which provided different leverage, and Sam entered her completely. He let out a low growl. "It's like being weight-less. Like being underwater but not having the resistance of it." Hazel's breath became choppy as she spoke.

Sam grabbed her hips and tipped her slightly back, she placed her hands on the bed, and he ravished her. His dick was so hard, and he felt a warm tingling in his face. Hazel's muscles started to contract around him again, and she gasped for air as she ground back against him. The tingling spread down his neck and chest and reached up to his ears. He was overwhelmed with the wave of release and howled as he came. Hazel exclaimed her satisfaction, and it sounded like a song in his ears.

They stilled. Sam's vision returned to focus, and he chortled at the sight of them. Hazel in the swing, his cock still in her, both of them, the swing, and their bed covered in paint. Hazel giggled too, and he loosed his grasp on her and let her swing back over the bed. "That was fun." he breathed.

"You liked?" She asked. Then, "How do I get out of this thing?"

Sam stepped forward and helped her out while answer-ing. "No. No, I didn't like it. It was incredible. And this," he shook the empty swing, "is amazing."

Hazel chuckled. "I thought so too! I'm sorry I couldn't give it to you at Christmas. I felt bad about that, but I couldn't imagine you opening any of this in front of your folks."

Sam leaned back into a deep reverie, imagining it. "I am happy to wait for delivery."

CHAPTER
NINE

"Holidays are joyful, there's always something new. But every day's a holiday, when I'm near to you."

HAZEL HAD SOMEHOW FOUND a matching set of intricate fox-inspired masquerade masks. Hers was a light orange and tan, with coppery swirls and spirals. His was similar but darker-hued, and the spirals were more prominent and not as curvy. There was no two ways about it, though; they were hot. Sam watched Hazel as she checked herself in the mirror. She was wearing her go-to little back dress and heels. The eyeholes in the mask were large enough that the time she spent on getting her smoky shadow done was not in vain.

Sam wolf-whistled at her. Hazel turned to him, smirking, and he apologized, "Sorry, I'm not sure how to fox whistle."

"You look incredible too." Sam had rented a classic slim-fitting tuxedo for the occasion, it was a little tight on his shoulders and arms, but he knew what Hazel liked on him. Hazel dug through her closet, "I love this look, but I'm going to freeze! Do you think they'll have the radiant heaters up there?"

"Probably, but you might have to engage in battle with other scantily clad persons for a good position."

She popped her head out of the door. "I can take them."

Sam held his hands up. "Don't hurt 'em too much."

Hazel dove back into the closet and pulled out a long black button-down jacket. "This'll get me up there. Then, we find and secure positions next to the heaters." Hazel's phone buzzed, and she exclaimed at it, then brought it to Sam to see. Rosie messaged a picture of her and Nick to them, they had matching masks too, but they were going as a doe and stag. Hazel crooned, "They look so good! This is going to be so much fun!"

Sam felt the little velvety box in his inner coat pocket. When they counted in the New Year, he would kiss her, then bend down on one knee. There was no better way to start the year; they'd be with their two best friends at a fantastic party in a beautiful place.

Finding parking in downtown Crestwood on New Year's Eve was a challenge. Sam snagged a spot at the library; they'd need to hoof it a few blocks to get to the party. However, the walk turned out to be a blessing because Crestwood was at its finest. Street musicians were on every corner, and the city was alive. Despite the biting midwinter cold and the grayness of the season, the people out celebrating energized the air with promise. Sam felt buoyant as they walked down the street.

Hazel shouted above the noisy crowd, "We haven't

talked about resolutions yet this year. Are you making any?"

Sam thought for a moment. "I guess we should resolve to be the best damned godparents anyone has ever had."

Hazel squeezed his hand. "That is a good one. We will spoil the child! Maybe we should get a bassinet or something, so they know they can come over anytime and have a place for the little one to sleep." Hazel started to speak again, hesitated, then said quickly, "I'm scared we won't see them as much."

Sam helped clear a path through a knot of people. When they were back beside each other, he asked, "You think their having a baby will change our friendship?"

"Yes. I mean, I know it will. It makes sense. They'll want family time alone, won't be as free to do game nights or go out, and will be tired at first, too. I expect that; I just don't want it to change in a bad way. You know? Like grow apart or anything."

Sam hummed. "Can I offer a counter-perspective?" Hazel nodded, and they both stopped walking as they arrived at their destination. "What if the changes bring us closer together? Maybe we see them a little less, but also, we are a part of family time. We'll see the baby grow into a kid and then an adult, and we'll be there every step of the way. Maybe they're more tired at first, and we can relieve them so they rest and we get baby time by ourselves. I imagine that we become even closer family than we already are." He leaned close to her ear and whispered, "I imagine when we have a baby, it will be best friends with theirs."

Hazel carefully ran a finger beneath her eye. "You're going to mess up my makeup! This is my curse, though; I always cry when I wear mascara... That's an amazing counter-perspective. Thank you."

"Anytime, Hazelberry."

They waited beside a lamp post, Hazel jumping in place to keep warm. Ten minutes had passed when Sam's phone buzzed in his pocket. "It's Nick."

Nick

> Guys, I am so sorry, but I don't think we're going to make it. 10:15pm

Nick

> Rosie has morning sickness, at night go figure, but it's been 30 minutes now and it's not getting better. Plus I can tell she's exhausted. 10:15pm

Nick

> I can still run the tickets out to you so you can get in. 10:16pm

HAZEL LEANED OVER THE PHONE, watching the texts come in. "Aw man, poor Rosie. I don't want to go without them. That would be weird right?"

> Oh no! We both hope she feels better soon, please send our love. Don't worry about the tickets, we'll get into something else.
> 10:16pm

"Yeah seems a bit weird to be at a company party without any relationship with anyone there or the company. I'd feel awful if he left Rosie to come do anything, too." Sam wouldn't let it show, but the hopeful bubble he'd been in on the way here had popped. If Hazel's curse was wearing mascara, then maybe his was intending to propose. Every time he tried, something went spectacularly wrong.

Hazel agreed, "Fair point. Honestly, I'm sure Rosie told him to. Well… what now?" She glanced up and down the street.

"I don't know. Most places are either closed or booked. We could walk around and see what's open."

They set off back the way they came, but as Sam predicted, most small businesses were closed for the night. Only the bars remained open, and they were packed. They dared to enter The Biergarten to escape the cold for a few minutes. It was standing room only, and they had to struggle to the bar to make an order. Hazel looked at the menu, scoffed, and said, "We can't stay here long. Three dollars for a PBR?! There's no way."

Sam was tall enough that he leaned through the crowd to call the bartender. "Sangria and a Gin and Tonic, please." The woman behind the counter turned to make their drinks, and Sam replied, "No doubt. I'm sure it's because of all of this." He indicated the mass of people.

Sam paid, and they sipped their drinks, standing in a slightly less densely populated corner.

"It's not even a good sangria!" Hazel exclaimed and chuckled at her plight.

"Luckily, there's no way to mess up a G&T."

Even in the corner, they were bumped into countless times and had trouble hearing each other. They stayed a short time before agreeing to brave the cold once more.

Back on the street, nothing was better off than The Biergarten, and eventually, they found their way back to the car. Hazel sat in the passenger seat, holding her hands to the heater with a twisted pout on her face. "It doesn't seem right to go home. It's New Year's; we're already out and dressed up…."

Sam put the car into drive. "You know what we haven't done in a long time? Drive the parkway at night."

"That is… perfect."

The Blue Ridge Parkway is a protected, slow-paced drive offering stunning views of the surrounding mountains and access to countless hiking areas. Sam had grown to love it immediately. During the day, the views were breathtaking, and the hiking rivaled some of his favorite spots growing up. At night, it was completely different. There were far fewer cars and no unnatural lights. The few sounds were of wildlife, and the stars spread gloriously across the inky sky. He and Hazel often took nighttime rides here. They had deep conversations or thought through things that were harder to tackle in the light of day but somehow easier to comprehend here, where it was slower and connected.

Sam pulled onto the parkway with no destination in mind. He was happy to be here to think and decompress from another proposal attempt gone awry. Hazel turned on an old Panic at the Disco album to which they could belt every word. Neither was a remarkably talented singer, but they sang together all the same.

Dense leafless trees were on both sides of the road; the darkness was only relieved when the trees gave way to a bare overlook. Then the distant pinpricks of light from towns and cities below stole their eyes. They drove through a mountain tunnel, and Sam stopped on the other side. A family of five deer were in the road, staring at the car. Hazel reached across the car and grabbed Sam's wrist. "Are you kidding me?"

"It doesn't seem real, does it?" Sam turned down the volume. The deer stood still for several moments, no movement aside from the flicking of tails, then the largest of them leapt to the other side. The other four followed, and they all disappeared into the foliage.

Hazel loosed a breath. "That was so cool."

They continued the slow trek for a few miles before approaching an overlook that exposed the city of Creswood. Sam pulled in and turned off the lights, which made the city shine even brighter. Hazel broke the silence. "It's beautiful. Crazy to think we were just down there amongst that glow." She sighed and weaved her fingers through his. "Know what I love?"

Sam replied immediately, "Page turners, rainbow trout, the feel of a warm cup in your hands on a cold day, anything fuzzy, wordplay, the thing on your phone that converts voicemail into a text, pu-erh. You're welcome for that one."

"Mmm, I do love those things, and now I want tea, but that wasn't what I was going to say." Hazel shook her head. "I love us. We're just good, you know? Everything is so easy, and nothing can get us down, even when things go wrong. Like tonight, our plans get canceled last minute, but we don't dwell; we head to the parkway. I feel so grateful for it and… secure. I know we're going to make it because there is nothing we can't overcome."

She squeezed his hand, and Sam squeezed back. Sam let her words steep in him. Hazel was right. In the time they'd been together, he could think of disappointments, cancelations, certainly changes in plans and unexpected events. He recalled the FutureApp Internship Program he'd been advocating to participate in for years getting turned down yet again- he really believed this was the year Communications would finally participate. He was disappointed and stunned to learn he was wrong. Hazel snuck out early that day to get ingredients for his favorite pumpkin risotto and made him dinner from scratch. She listened to him recount the entire story and vent his frustrations over the rice, then helped him plan a new approach for this year. When they'd flown out to visit Portland, they had a terrible time with flight cancelations and delays. They ended up spending an entire day stuck in the Atlanta Airport. Sam made a playlist of songs and collected snacks from vendors, while Hazel made a massive list of two-player games. They'd eaten chocolate truffles and gummy worms and played games with an EarPod in one of their ears each all day.

Fireworks exploded across the sky above the city. Hazel clapped and checked her phone. "Ah! What a view! It's midnight! Happy New Year!"

Sam leaned over the center console and kissed Hazel. He held the back of her head in his palm and used the other hand to stroke down the side of her face. The crushing realization of how stupid he had been lasted a second before his chest seemed to expand past his body. Sam had never felt so full of pure appreciation. When their kiss ended, he said, "Let's go outside to watch."

They stood facing the fireworks, side by side, Hazel's head resting on his shoulder. Sam could feel his heart beating down through the soles of his feet. "Hazel. I've been an idiot." He laughed. "For a while now, I've been trying to give you something perfect. The best possible experience, because you deserve that. You deserve everything good. But it didn't occur to me that every day is perfect because we have each other even when things go sideways. We roll with anything thrown our way. Each day we're together is the best day. I love that about us too." He wrapped his fingers around the box in his pocket and gently stepped into a kneel.

Time slowed down. He could see her face, fireworks bathing her in different colors, flashes reflected in her eyes. Sam opened the box and held it out to her. "I want to have the best day with you, every day, for the rest of my life." Tears were shining on her cheeks, but she was smiling. Hazel had never looked so lovely. "Will you marry me?"

It seemed hard for Hazel to speak, but he saw her swallow, and she answered, "Yes." Then she turned toward the overlook and yelled it at the top of her lungs. "Yes! Yes! Forever yes!" She pulled him up by his hands. Sam was filled with such energy that he picked her up, spun her around, and lowered her into a kiss.

EPILOGUE

"Good tidings we bring to you and your kin. We wish you a Merry Christmas and a Happy New Year."

THE FIRST CROCUSES had pushed through the earth to announce the coming of Spring. Hazel thought it was still plenty cold at the moment as she saw her breath hang in the air. She and Sam had returned from a morning run around their neighborhood. It was a normal day, except they had set it aside to formally start planning the wedding, something she had never done. Even when she was engaged to Alex, no effort had been put into planning the event. Hazel almost wished she had a "dream wedding" from her childhood she could use to build from. Not having a vision gave her too many options, which made her overwhelmed with decisions. Sam was in the same boat, which is how they decided to have a dedicated planning day in the first place. Rosie and Nick would join them to help with ideas after their doctor's appointment.

They showered off, made breakfast, and shuffled the

bridal magazines and color swatches to make room on the table to sit. Hazel took a bite of toast and asked, "Where do we start? Location? Colors? Guests?"

"Location, right? Because I feel like it could inform colors and guests."

"Ooo, or the date, because the date might inform the location! We wouldn't want a beach wedding in January."

Sam pointed at her. "Good call. I like that. Okay, date."

"One idea would be to keep it around our anniversary. Mid-November-ish." Hazel suggested.

Rosie's voice came to them from the living room. "You know your door was open? Anyway, don't do June because we officially have our due date on June 18th!" She took off her coat, draping it over a chair, and Nick swept behind her placing his hands over her baby bump and kissing her neck.

Hazel cheered, "Aw, yay! That's the perfect time to be born. Amazing! How'd the appointment go?"

Nick slid a sonogram image across the table to them; he couldn't stop smiling. "Everything is perfect. Baby is healthy. Mom is healthy." He rubbed Rosie's neck.

Rosie rolled her eyes. "And Dad is… pre-nesting? Is that a thing? I swear he offered to shave my legs last night. He won't let me do anything!"

Nick plopped into the seat next to her. "I just want to be involved. It's hard being the Dad. It's like you get to do all the awesome bonding parts, have our baby inside of you, and I'm some dope on the outside."

"Nick, you are going to be such a great Dad. Your time is coming." Hazel assured him.

Sam was looking at him thoughtfully. "I've never thought about that before, but I think I get it."

Nick shook his head. "It's the worst, man. I just want to

help and be part of this baby's life so bad. It's like I have all this energy and nowhere to put it."

Rosie squeezed Nick's knee and then shot her eyes back to Hazel. "This is all well and good, but it isn't the topic we're tackling! You were figuring out the date, and we eliminated June. I'd also vote to nix July while I'm at it. I'm planning to be exhausted for the full month." She winked at Hazel and Sam.

"And I'm not totally sold on November," Sam added, "I do like the idea of keeping our anniversary, but we always have the summit in November. As long as we're at FutureApp, we'll have to be there."

Hazel put the pen she was holding to her mouth and twirled it around. "October might work if we want to get married this year. If we want to wait until next year, we could also do Springtime. It depends on how big it will be and how much planning time we need."

Rosie laughed, and everyone turned attention to her. "I'm sorry, but you two are funny. You don't want a big wedding. Actually, the reason you're having issues planning this thing is that neither of you cares much about the wedding. You care about the marriage. Which is exactly how it should be! Do it in October. Make it simple."

Hazel saw Sam turn to her, and she met his gaze. "She's right," he said.

"She's always unnervingly right." Hazel agreed.

Rosie shrugged. "It's a blessing and a curse, I'm afraid." In this case, it was a blessing. The rest of the planning seemed to take care of itself. They checked the calendar and agreed on Friday, October 6th. Western North Carolina would be experiencing fine weather at that time, and the autumn leaves would make for beautiful scenery, so they decided to have a small ceremony locally and outdoors.

They discussed colors and searched the internet for

venue options. They boggled that the baby would be nearly four months old by then.

There were more decisions to make. Hazel knew flowers, dresses, food, music, and officiants were all in her future, but she had an idea now. It was more like filling in those blanks than writing the tale from scratch, which was infinitely doable. She realized, looking around the table at her friends- her family- while she had never dwelled on a dream wedding, she had imagined a dream life. This was it.

AFTERWORD

Dear Reader,

The fact that you exist is wild to me. Thank you for taking a chance on me. I am humbled.

If you want a little more, something of a bonus prologue is available for your enjoyment! You can get Sam's Vow here- bit.ly/LocallyBonus or scan below.

If you enjoyed this novella, please consider leaving a review or checking out *Remotely Love* to dive into Hazel and Sam's story.

Happy Reading!

Acknowledgments

Locally Love was a surprise even to me.

I had the idea floating around that I wanted to write a holiday novella and an inkling I may not be done with the characters from *Remotely Love,* who I adore. The thoughts didn't collide until one fateful day in the early summer of 2023. What an aha moment that was!

Thank you to Tim Thorn, who assured me I could write it in time to publish for the holiday season. You used math to prove your point, and I was reminded how much I love you in those moments.

Heather Balcerek, instead of politely declining, celebrated when I asked if she would be interested in doing another cover for me. She is an absolute queen and helps me with everything else, too!

My beta readers (Tim Thorn, Heather Balcerek, Alyssa Westler, and Steve Cahill) have unwittingly become my "beta team." I adore you. Your feedback pushes me to improve as a writer, and you are undoubtedly related to any success I ever experience.

My family has been a constant support for my writing journey. I thank you all.

And to you. Thank you for reading my book.

ABOUT THE AUTHOR

Lori Thorn is the author of Remotely Love: A work from home romance.

Lori draws inspiration from her life, including working remotely for major corporations since 2012. She lives in Florida with her husband, Tim, and their three kiddos. She enjoys playing in the community band and preparing scrumptious vegetarian meals.

ABOUT THE ILLUSTRATOR

Heather Balcerek is a passionate creative and lover of books. While her design experience has been born out of necessity in her past roles, she eagerly learns new programs and tricks of the trade whenever she can. Whether she is drawing Zentangles or noodling around on ProCreate or designing in Canva, Heather puts all her love and energy into each piece. Aside from visual creativity, she also hosts the Connect the Dots, Lead the Way podcast. which focuses on leadership development.

Heather lives in Clearwater, FL with her husband. Together they run the food and travel blog, It's a Salty Life.

Connect with Heather

@msheatherbdot
  (https://www.instagram.com/msheatherbdot/)

Find her podcast and more at ThePolkaDotDesk.com.

@saltylifefft
  (https://www.instagram.com/saltylifefft/)

itsasaltylife.com
  (https://www.itsasaltylife.com)

Matchmaking
Cats
of the
Goddesses

WELCOME TO
HELL'S B&B

Satan's Kitty

Satan's Kitty

A PAWSITIVELY PURRFECT MATCH MADE IN HELL

PEPPER MCGRAW

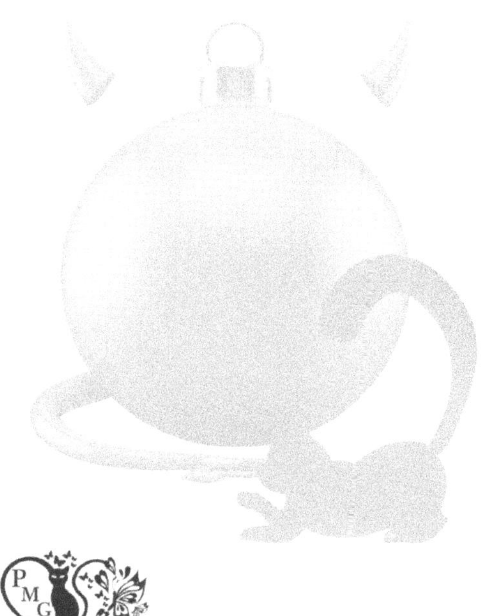

Contents

One

THAT BYGUL'S LATEST matchmaking efforts resulted in Christmas morning dawning at the Bed & Breakfast in Hell *wasn't* his fault.

He was the top matchmaking cat at Pawsitively Purrfect Matches, for goddess' sake. He was a professional and he didn't make mistakes like that.

He blamed Soraya.

Ever since she saw Jasmine playing with the kittens at the witches' coven house in Zero, Kansas, all Soraya could talk about was matching that little girl with one of the kittens on their caseload *and* matching a mate for her mother, who was both human and single.

Bygul kept reminding Soraya that neither Starlight

nor her daughter, Jasmine, were on their caseload, but this didn't matter to Soraya.

"Witches first," Bygul kept saying, "especially after we lost weeks in Jamesville, matching Tempest's sister."

But then, catastrophe struck, no pun intended.

Jasmine wrote a letter to Santa, but before anyone could read it, the letter disappeared and Starlight went into a tizzy, begging her daughter to tell her what she'd asked Santa for.

Jasmine, being the stubborn sort, refused to share. "It's magic, Mom. Magic took the letter to Santa and Santa's gonna take care of everything, so don't worry."

The problem was that Bygul assumed Soraya had stolen the letter, so that she could get details that might help her choose the purrfect kitten for Jasmine.

Soraya assumed Tivali stole the letter for the same reason.

None of them suspected the demon hell-cat, Kyrie.

Unfortunately, being a hell-cat, Kyrie had a lot of magic herself and could pretty much zip around Zero however she pleased.

And apparently, she pleased to steal that letter.

Luc was bored.

He hated to admit it, but now that both his daughters were living in the Earth realm, there just wasn't as much excitement in Hell anymore.

Merry wasn't picking fights with demons on a daily basis.

Tempest wasn't causing cyclones of fire.

Merry wasn't riling up the pixies and causing wars.

Tempest wasn't raging at him to stop sending demons to court her.

It really was too quiet and too calm around Hell now that they were gone.

"Mrawr." One of the hell-kitties bumped her head against his leg.

"Yes, thank you, darling. I'm okay, just missing my girls. Who knew after all those years tearing out my hair, attempting to stop Tempest from chasing the flames of hell with her tornadoes and storms, that I would actually miss the chaos she wrought?

"That little girl was a menace from the very beginning, tormenting the flames of hell from her toddler days. I'd be racing to the borders of Hell, barely making it in time to yank the flames back into one of our realms, and you know what she'd be doing while I was busy chasing chaos?"

"Mrawr." Another hell-cat leapt onto the arm of his chair and bonked his cheek with his nose.

"That's right. She'd laugh! She'd just plop down wherever we were, surrounded by flames, and laugh and laugh while I ran around like an idiot, chasing those flames she'd fanned to epic heights.

"Me! Satan, the Prince of Darkness, Lord of the Nine Realms of Hell, and The Beast, chasing after a bunch of renegade flames from Hell. She did it on purpose. Riling them up. And as bad as she was, when Merry came along, oh, that little girl turned me old before my time."

A third cat leapt onto the back of his chair and stretched out along the top of it, settling her head on his left shoulder. "I'm telling you, I discovered my first gray hair two days after Merry's arrival here. I was spending every moment of my day desperately trying to keep all those demons from attacking my baby girl.

"I mean, can you imagine? Two years old and she was riling up thousand-year-old demons, with just one look. Just one look."

Luc fell silent as he remembered that mischievous look on her face.

She'd taken total, unequivocal delight in sending the calmest of demons stark, raving mad.

He chuckled. "She owned my heart from that very first moment." He sighed. "I really thought things would be better without them here, knowing they were safer in another realm, but now? Now I'd give anything to have them both back, causing mayhem and turning my hair gray."

ALL STARLIGHT EVER WANTED WAS A NORMAL life.

It was really quite unfortunate that normal just wasn't in the cards for her.

First, she was born to vagabonds.

They liked to claim they were hippies, but that was just ridiculous.

Vagabonds who traveled everywhere was what they truly were.

She wasn't sure how they did it, given they seemed as human as humans could get, but her dad, in particular, had a talent for finding portals and other crossings between the realms and would just lead the way through, sauntering from one realm to the next.

"We're off on another adventure, Starlight!" He would exclaim, right before dragging them into a realm ruled entirely by fire-breathing dragons.

Yeah. Thanks, Dad.

Under normal circumstances—again, if she'd had a normal life—when Starlight turned eighteen, she would have struck out on her own.

The only problem was, her eighteenth birthday dawned in the troll realm, where they were trapped.

Not because the trolls were evil or anything.

No.

It was just that her dad got them thoroughly lost and refused to ask for directions.

Five years later, right around her twenty-third birthday, they *finally* found another realm crossing, but at that point, they were about thirty realms away from the entrance to Earth.

Starlight was actually starting to believe her parents were doing it on purpose, just to keep her with them a little longer, when finally, *finally,* they made it back to the earth realm.

Twenty-one years later.

She'd left earth as a toddler, with occasional visits back, every couple years, then nothing for almost thirty.

Forty-four years old and still traveling with her parents.

That was more than enough information to explain *all* of the events that followed.

Their last realm-move involved traversing between Shenanigans.

Starlight was always thrilled when a crossing involved one Shenanigans, let alone two or more.

Sometimes, it was a hotel, sometimes a bed and breakfast, sometimes it was just a raggedy-looking bar, but if there was a Shenanigans anywhere in sight, it signified safety.

It was years before Starlight understood that it was unusual for humans to be able to access a Shenanigans. They were all built as safe zones for paranormals, which meant that humans weren't supposed to be able to even see them.

Except Starlight and her parents could.

Of course, whenever she pointed out that they must not be human and asked what type of paranormal they were, her parents just shrugged and said, "But we *are* humans, darling. That's all we've ever been."

Whatever.

So they didn't want to tell her, that was fine.

Besides, pretending to be human meant Starlight could also pretend to be normal.

That never lasted long, of course, but at least she tried.

In any case, when they *finally* arrived back on earth and Starlight realized a Hotel Shenanigans was waiting for them there, even though it was the most run-down Shenanigans hotel she'd ever seen, she immediately insisted they stay the night.

Her parents tried to convince her to stay on the fairy side of the hotel, but Starlight wasn't falling for that. Oh, no.

She'd been realm-walking her entire life and now that she was back in the earth realm, she planned to stay.

For a long while.

"But no one's really running this side of the hotel, darling," her mother protested.

"The bar is open," Starlight said, "and the leprechaun bartender told me he'd rent me a room if I wanted one. So I'm staying here. In the earth realm."

"You can't trust leprechauns, you know that," her father said.

"It's not nice to repeat stereotypes," Starlight said.

"It's not a stereotype when it's true," her father countered.

Starlight just glared at him.

Her mother sighed, then said in a long-suffering voice, "Very well, darling. We'll be on the fairy side if you need us." She waited, but when Starlight said nothing, she added, "We'll see you in the morning then."

Starlight waited until her parents boarded the elevator, its doors closed and the arrow above them slowly moved over to hover between the numbers two and three before stopping there.

She waited a bit longer to be sure they wouldn't be coming back down, then made a beeline for the bar where she celebrated her return to her birth realm by getting drunk and having sex.

Lots and lots of sex.

Two months later, when she turned up pregnant, she couldn't express even a little bit of surprise.

This was what happened when you were completely irresponsible, right?

Unfortunately, due to the drinking, she had absolutely no idea who the father was.

In fact, she didn't remember a thing about that night, other than the flashes of heat that came anytime she tried to remember.

That was something at least.

She had no memories, but she was pretty certain a good time had been had by all.

Not remembering the details meant she couldn't inform the father when she found out she was pregnant, and perhaps that was a blessing because it meant when Jasmine was born, Starlight didn't have to share her with anyone.

Not even her parents because they were most definitely not done with the realm-hopping.

Of course, they tried to convince Starlight to travel with them.

"You can have a baby anywhere," her mother exclaimed. "I did!"

"Even better," her father said, "You can *raise* a child anywhere. We did!"

Yes. She was quite aware of the fact that it was possible to drag a child from realm to realm for her entire lifetime. She might dispute the use of the word "raise" though.

Of course, Starlight didn't say that because it would have hurt her parents' feelings and for all their faults, they did love her.

They just loved traveling more.

Which meant, that once they accepted that Starlight was serious when she said her traveling days were over, they said their goodbyes and hit the road.

At the time, they were in a tiny town called Zero, Kansas.

They'd been on their way to California when Starlight had a bout of morning sickness, and so, it was in Zero, Kansas, that she discovered she was pregnant with Jasmine.

It was also in Zero, Kansas, that Starlight decided to stay.

She fell in love with the town almost immediately.

It was as close to a ghost town as one could get.

The sign on the outskirts of town proclaimed a population of fifty-nine, which increased to sixty-two when Starlight and her parents arrived, then fell to sixty when her parents resumed their travels. Several months later, that number jumped to sixty-one when Jasmine was born.

A lot of people would be horrified to live in a town that was so empty and quiet, but for Starlight, that emptiness and silence was what she craved.

A tiny pocket of normal in her otherwise crazy life.

There were no Shenanigans in sight, which reduced the likelihood of paranormals or realm crossings being anywhere around.

Best of all, there was absolutely nothing in Zero, Kansas, that threatened Starlight's dream of normalcy for herself, and *most* especially, for the daughter she planned to raise there.

She mostly got her wish.

Life was pretty normal for the next ten years.

Starlight worked as a waitress at Zero Diner, while Jasmine went to school a couple towns over with seven other children from Zero.

Of course, every so often, Starlight would get a reminder of her crazy past, when a postcard would arrive from her parents, or worse, when they would show up to regale her and Jasmine with tales of the latest realms they'd visited.

Starlight worried their stories would make Jasmine wish for a different life, to travel the realms like Starlight had with her parents, but so far, Jasmine seemed happy with her life in Zero, Kansas, and that made Starlight happy as well.

Then, out of nowhere, everything changed.

First, a coven of witches moved to town, then they cast a spell—a stupid, idiotic spell for their fated mates—and the next thing Starlight knew, there were paranormals everywhere.

Everywhere!

Seven witches and they caused all this chaos.

First, a wolf pack moved in, then a Vampire Coven showed up, followed by a coalition of Chameleons.

Suddenly, Starlight's perfectly normal life, was as crazy as it had ever been.

Her shifts at the diner were now the opposite of normal.

Every. Single. Day.

Shifters bursting into wolf form.

Chameleons planning heists and outrageous cons right in the middle of the diner.

Witches starting fires and raising the dead.

Then, there was the vampire.

The infuriating, sexy, know-it-all, devastatingly handsome vampire, Talon.

She'd done an amazing job of ignoring him every time he came into the diner, even while serving him. She ignored his flirting, pretended her heart didn't race every time he got near and that the sound of his gravely voice didn't send shivers down her spine.

She got really good at pretending.

Then the shy witch lost control of her sex magic one day and the next thing Starlight knew, she was over the vampire's shoulder, being carted out.

She was lucky he was so impatient and only took her to the side alley, where he pressed her up against the wall and proceeded to turn her brain to mush.

She'd *never*, in all her fifty-four years, been kissed like that.

Or if she had, the kisses were lost with all the other memories of that night, and even if they hadn't been, they'd have been obliterated, along with every other thought in her head, from the heat that blazed through her from Talon's kiss.

She was seconds from spontaneous combustion when the school bus lumbered around the corner.

Saved by her daughter.

Jasmine was dropped off outside the diner every afternoon at four o'clock sharp and it was only the sound of the bus as it pulled into the town square that brought Starlight back to her senses.

She'd avoided the vampire ever since, though it was hard to do when he was always coming into her place of employment and flirting with her, but she did her best.

Of course, avoiding him during the day would have been so much easier if the rumors of vampires and sunlight were true. However, as it turned out, the severe sunburns caused by a witch's curse were only inconvenient and painful, rather than deadly.

Perhaps it was a bit selfish that Starlight lamented this fact occasionally, but she couldn't help it. After all, the vampire not only made a pest of himself at the diner during the days, but was also a constant visitor in her disturbingly vivid dreams at night.

It felt as if that kiss had awakened something inside, and not just her libido, but a feeling she couldn't quite grasp, one of familiarity and extreme deja vu.

It was as if she knew the feel of his lips before they connected with hers, the way he would lift her closer, the way his arms would wrap so tightly around her, the way his hand would come up to cradle her head, even the way he would taste.

She'd been living in fear ever since.

Wondering.

Was it possible this vampire she'd wanted from the minute she'd seen him was a memory she'd forgotten?

Could she have had the terminal bad luck of moving to a town where ten years later, her daughter's father would also move? And was it fair for her to keep her suspicions to herself? To not give her daughter the chance to know the man who might actually be her father?

But what if Starlight was wrong?

These were the questions that kept her awake at night, worrying.

Lately though, Starlight had much bigger worries to consume her thoughts at night.

Like what her daughter had put into her letter to

Santa Claus. At this point, the situation had become critical.

In the past, Jasmine would hand her letter to Starlight, who would post it to Santa Claus. After reading it, of course.

This year, though, the letter went missing.

Jasmine insisted it was in Santa's hands and not to worry.

Starlight had tried to get her to write another letter, just in case, but Jasmine had refused, which left Starlight completely in the dark.

And now, it was Christmas Eve and there was nothing more Starlight could do.

If Jasmine had asked for anything other than a kitten, Starlight was screwed.

"I HAVE GOOD NEWS AND BAD NEWS," SORAYA announced as she arrived.

Bygul laid back his ears in annoyance. Seriously? More bad news? "All right. Let's hear it."

"The good news is that I found the letter."

"Well, thank goodness," Tivali said. "Santa Kitty

had it, didn't he? That pompous, arrogant fleabag just can't help himself! What's he up to now?"

"Well, that's also—kind of—the good news. Santa Kitty *doesn't* have the letter."

"Well, thank goodness," Tivali muttered. "If I had to spend another Christmas with that cat, I don't know what I'd do."

"That's also kind of the bad news," Soraya said. "Because Satan has it."

A HELL-CAT LEAPT ONTO LUC'S LAP, startling him and making him chuckle. "Well, now, when did you get here, Kyrie? Did you get bored in the earth realm already? How's my sweet girl, Tempest, doing?"

Kyrie let out a happy meow and started making biscuits on his legs, causing Luc to yelp and laugh again.

"Okay, okay." He stroked her over and over again until her purr rumbled through the room like a freight train.

Over the next thirty minutes, one by one, Kyrie's

kittens, who were no longer kitten-sized, jumped onto Luc's lap to climb all over their mother, batting at her tail and chewing on her ears, until Kyrie lost her patience, slammed a paw on the offending kitten's neck and pinning them down, groomed them to her satisfaction. Eventually, she lifted her paw and the kitten ran away, only to be replaced with another one.

Luc chuckled when he realized that some of the kittens visiting weren't Kyrie's at all. Still she tolerated their play, then groomed each one until the visits finally tapered off.

At that point, Kyrie curled up into a ball and napped for a while.

Of course, during this time, Luc had no choice but to remain motionless, frozen in his chair, a victim of feline purralysis.

Luc felt a terrible mix of both relief and profound regret, when Kyrie finally stood, stretching leisurely before butting her head against his and jumping down.

"Thanks for visiting, Kyrie," Luc called after her. "We miss you around here."

With a swish of her tail and head held high, Kyrie sauntered from the room.

It was only when she was completely gone that Luc realized she'd left something behind. "What's this?"

An envelope sat on his lap.

It was addressed to Satan Claus, North Pole, from a Jasmine in Zero, Kansas.

Luc chuckled. "Haven't received one of these in a long time, now have we, kittens? Ever since the humans automated everything, most of the misspelled letters still make it to good old Mr. Claus. Well, let's see what we can do for Miss Jasmine of Zero, Kansas."

He opened the letter, scanned it and laughed. "Oh, this is going to be sooo much fun."

Two

"DID YOU *KNOW* this was going to happen?" Bygul demanded.

"Of course not!" Soraya wailed. "I knew Jasmine wrote a letter to Santa, but I thought Kitty Claus stole it. I mean, that *is* kind of his job, collecting all the unposted letters for Santa."

"Oh, please," Muezza said. "When has that lazy cat ever done his job?"

"You guys all thought the same," Soraya said. "I know you did."

"Guilty," Tivali said. "I was *really* dreading the thought of him returning. You know how incompetent he is."

"Yes, well, this situation is much worse than K.C.'s

incompetence," Bygul said severely. "Does anyone have *any* idea what that letter says?"

"I tried to take a peek when Satan was reading it, but his hell-cats kept getting in the way." Soraya twitched her ears in annoyance. "The only word I managed to see was kitten."

"Well, that's not so bad," Muezza said. "Maybe we can manipulate which kitten Satan gives her for Christmas. We've got plenty on the caseload."

"Are you being serious right now?" Tivali demanded.

"What?"

"*Satan*? Lord of the Nine Realms of Hell?"

"So?"

"Infamous hell-cat daddy?"

"Oh. Shit."

"Exactly," Bygul said morosely. "What do you think are the chances of him choosing an *appropriate* kitten for a nine-year-old human?"

"Zero," the other cats chorused.

"Mama, Mama!"

"Five more minutes, baby," Starlight murmured, not even opening her eyes. She'd been up until two wrapping gifts for Jasmine's stocking and wrestling the cat tree into position beside the real tree.

She'd then gotten the brilliant idea to try and wrap the stupid thing.

She'd finally given up and just fashioned a bow for it instead.

"But Mama, my wishes came true!"

Oh, thank goodness. Jasmine must have peeked and seen the cat tree, which meant she really *had* asked for a kitten for Christmas.

"They're so sweet, Mama!"

They're?

"Mrawr."

Starlight's eyes flew open. She'd planned to take Jasmine to pick out her kitten the next day. There shouldn't already be one in the house.

"What are—where did? Jasmine!"

"Yeah, Mom?" Jasmine popped her head up over the side of the bed.

"What are you doing down there?" Starlight sat up and shoved her hair out of her face.

"Playing with the kittens. Look, Mom, aren't they adorable?" She popped back up with two kittens in her arms. They were both pitch black, though one had white paws.

Where in the world had *they* come from?

Starlight sighed.

No doubt she had her parents to blame for this.

They'd probably popped in just long enough to leave a couple kittens, then popped out again.

Either that or they'd stayed and were even now camping out in her guest room or cooking breakfast in the kitchen.

She grimaced.

Oh, well.

There was nothing she could do about it now.

They were here and so were the kittens and Jasmine was on cloud nine.

Starlight supposed it could be worse.

She could have already gotten a kitten and then there'd be three in the house. Plus—bonus—she no longer had to drive two towns over to adopt one.

She stood, reached for her robe and froze.

How she'd failed to notice that more kittens than expected was the least of her problems was a huge mystery, but she was definitely noticing now.

Despite having gone to sleep in her own bedroom, she now stood somewhere else entirely.

"Jasmine. Do you know where we are right now?"

"Uh-huh. We're in a bed and breakfast."

"A bed and—" Shit.

Starlight knew *exactly* what was happening.

She knew it!

It had happened entirely too many times in her childhood for her not to recognize what this was.

They'd been realm-walked overnight in their sleep.

"Where are they?" She yanked her robe on and tied it shut with a few vicious jerks.

"Who?" Jasmine asked.

"Your grandparents."

"They're here?"

"Wait. You haven't seen them?"

Jasmine shook her head. "I've only seen Mrs. Butters and her kittens."

"Mrs. Butters?" Starlight asked faintly, before sinking back onto the bed.

One kitten.

She'd planned on *one* kitten. Not two and their mama.

She glanced around. The bedroom was beautiful and charming, with gorgeous, wooden furniture and intricate, crown moulding. "What the hell is going on?"

"My wishes came true, Mama."

"Okay, maybe it's time you told me what your wishes were."

"I wished for a kitten, of course, but Santa gave me seven plus a mama kitty."

"Seven?" Starlight whimpered, unable to even fathom the sheer chaos seven kittens could cause.

Not to mention the litter boxes.

Except, didn't Jasmine say this was a bed and breakfast?

Oh, thank goodness.

"You know, sweetheart, the cats probably all belong to the owner of this bed and breakfast, so you shouldn't get too attached."

"They don't, Mama! I know because Santa left me a letter telling me they were my Christmas present."

Starlight could honestly say that until that moment, she'd never had the urge to throat punch Santa Claus *or* to knee him in the groin. Now, it was all she could think about.

"Come on, Mama, the other kittens and my letter are in the living room."

"Okay, but hold on a minute. How do you even know this is a bed and breakfast?" Shit. Had Jasmine gone exploring in some alternate realm while Starlight had been sleeping?

"Because of my wishes, Mama. It's my present to

you. I mean, it's mostly from Santa, but it was my idea."

"I don't understand, darling."

"I asked for a vacation at a bed and breakfast because you love having breakfast in bed."

"Oh, well, that was really sweet of you, Jasmine, but—"

"Come see the rest of the kittens, Mama!" Jasmine grabbed her hand and dragged her out of the room she'd been sleeping in, down the hall and into a small living room, where all their Christmas decorations and presents were waiting.

The stockings Starlight had filled the night before were hanging from a small fireplace.

The Christmas tree she and Jasmine had decorated the day after Thanksgiving was shining bright in one corner and the cat tree Starlight had failed to wrap, stood tall with a bright red bow in the opposite corner.

"Aren't they wonderful?" Jasmine demanded from where she was lying on the ground, head under the Christmas tree.

That was when Starlight noticed the kittens.

Racing around the trunk of the Christmas tree, one broke free from the pack and charged across the room.

Several gave chase and then there were kittens

everywhere, batting at each other's tails, pouncing on each other, wrestling and tumbling over the floor.

"Come look, Mama!"

Starlight crouched down beside Jasmine and peeked under the tree.

There lay mama cat, a content look on her face, with two adorable kittens snuggled close.

Against her will, Starlight's heart melted a little.

"WELL, THIS IS A PERFECT NIGHTMARE," Bygul said.

"I mean the hell-kittens are kind of cute," Soraya said.

"Of course, they are. They're cats, aren't they?" Bygul said. "But that's not the point."

"What is the point?" TIvali asked.

"I don't even know," Bygul said. "We just need to get the humans back to the earth realm as soon as possible."

"But what if they're supposed to be there?" Soraya asked. "What if Starlight is Lucifer's mate?"

"I thought you were rooting for the vampire," Tivali said.

"Well, I *am*, but it's going to be difficult to match them when he's on Earth and she's in Hell."

"Actually, that's purrfect," Bygul said. "Someone just needs to let the vampire know that Satan kidnapped his mate. Problem solved, guaranteed."

"On it!" Soraya exclaimed and disappeared with a pop.

"That's a *terrible* plan," Tivali said, "or have you forgotten the feud between Talon's father and Satan?"

"Oh, I haven't forgotten," Bygul said. "I just don't have the patience for diplomacy when I'm back in Hell."

"*Back* in Hell?" Muezza exclaimed.

"When were you here before?" Tivali asked.

"Too recently for me to be happy about being back." Bygul hated thinking about that trip to the Underworld, mostly because he didn't remember all the details, something that was quite unusual for him.

He blamed Kalyn. Whenever things got particularly messy, it was usually because his brother was involved.

DECIDING TO JUST GO WITH THE FLOW WAS the best decision Starlight could have made for herself.

It was the mama cat who did it. Well, and Jasmine's absolute joy at being somewhere new, with kittens and her mom and no need for either to go to work or school the next day.

Starlight had no idea who had gifted them the stay at the B&B or who had sent them the mama cat and kittens, but she decided to be grateful.

Even if it turned out to be her parents or a paranormal or even Santa Claus, Starlight was going to be grateful.

Even though there was no snow on Christmas morning because upon stepping out onto the front porch of the B&B, they discovered they were standing along the outer edge of the Ninth Realm of Hell, Starlight was grateful.

Even though there were flames everywhere, and yes, she'd been forced into another realm with her daughter without her permission, Starlight decided to be grateful.

She was grateful because, at the end of the day, it

turned out that living in a bed and breakfast was the most amazing experience on earth.

Even though it wasn't exactly normal.

It had taken Starlight ten years to come to this conclusion, but a week spent at Hell's B&B, with a troll for a landlord and sweet kittens who occasionally morphed into giant hell-cats with fangs longer than her daughter's arm, but who would defend her with their lives, made Starlight realize that perhaps, just perhaps, normal was overrated.

Her very normal house back in the earth realm had never created for the two of them a room full of their favorite books, board games and puzzles, the way the B&B did, almost as if it were shaping itself to their desires.

Their home had never produced hot chocolate out of thin air when Jasmine mentioned she wished they had brought some with them. It had also never sprinkled marshmallows on top when Jasmine had clapped her hands and exclaimed delightedly, "And marshmallows please?"

Their house had never created a little girl's dream playroom that morphed occasionally to suit her mood and curiosity.

"The house likes you," Lekhleth, the troll running the B&B, told them.

"It does?" Jasmine exclaimed, wonder in her voice.

"Absolutely. It's never given *me* hot chocolate. If *I* want hot chocolate, I have to make it."

Jasmine giggled and Starlight wondered if that were true.

Was the house really that responsive to them or did it respond that way to all of its paying guests? Not that they were paying, of course, but she imagined *someone* had paid for their stay.

Lekhleth had gone on to confide that she was terribly homesick, which had led Starlight to ask what she missed the most, which had resulted in them spending hours bonding over their memories of the troll realm.

Since Starlight had spent five years there, following her parents as they searched for a crossing to take them elsewhere, she had many memories of all the places they'd visited.

"I miss it more and more every day," Lekhleth said. "It wouldn't be so bad if I enjoyed running the B&B, but I don't."

Starlight couldn't understand why since running the B&B seemed like the cushiest job ever.

Lekhleth received free room and board in this gorgeous home in exchange for making sure everything ran smoothly. She didn't have to actually clean the rooms or cook the meals—others took care of those chores. All she had to do was take people's money, smile and make them feel welcome.

Which, granted, probably wasn't the easiest thing to ask of a troll, given how antisocial they usually were.

Plus, she did have to manage the business end of things, paying the bills and doing payroll and all that, but it all sounded like a dream job to Starlight.

Which was why when Lekhleth asked if she wanted to be the manager instead, Starlight didn't hesitate to say yes.

"THIS IS A DISASTER," BYGUL EXCLAIMED. "Why didn't you stop her?"

"Why didn't you?" Tivali countered.

"It happened so fast. I had no idea she was going to ask that, and then before I could even react, Starlight had already said yes. Does she *know* what she's done?"

"Highly doubtful," Muezza said.

"This is terrible."

"I'm back!" Soraya exclaimed as she raced into the

room. "Good news! Talon's *furious* and he's coming as quickly as possible to rescue his mate!"

"No!" Bygul, Muezza and Tivali exclaimed all at once.

"What do you mean no? I thought that was the plan."

"Not anymore. She just committed to running the B&B," Bygul said.

"What?" Soraya exclaimed. "How could you let this happen?"

"We didn't know. It happened so fast," Tivali said.

"I don't know about you guys," Muezza said sourly, "but I have zero confidence this match is going to work out. In fact, I'm pretty sure it's doomed."

Three

TALON PACED BACK and forth furiously. "This is crazy. How can one woman and a little girl disappear and no one have seen a thing? It's Christmas, for fang's sake!"

"We've looked everywhere," Blade said. "They're just not in Zero anymore."

"Talon, son, you need to stay calm," Lassiter said. "We'll get to the bottom of this, I promise."

"Before they've been hurt or worse?"

Lassiter stepped into Talon's path, caught a hand behind his neck and pulled him close, pressing their foreheads together. "If someone hurts either one of them, we will reign the wrath of Hell upon them, I promise you that."

Talon closed his eyes, drew in a deep breath, then nodded. "I should be with her right now, Dad. I should have claimed her the minute I knew she was my mate."

"She's human and you gave her time. Time to adjust, to accept. You did nothing wrong, my son."

"I have a theory," Dinara said. "It doesn't really make sense, but—"

Talon's heart leapt in hope as he turned to his sister. "What is it?"

"Her parents are known realm-walkers. Perhaps the daughter is too."

"I've never seen any evidence that she's a traveler," Talon said slowly. "I'm also unaware of any realm crossings here in Zero."

"We should ask the witches," Lassiter said. "After all, we know they had a steady stream of visitors from the Hell realm a while back."

"Yes, but not all demons have to open a portal," Talon said. "Some just use the flames to travel."

"True," Dinara said, "but if even one of them can't access the flames—"

"They might have accidentally left open a portal," Talon said.

"Exactly," Dinara said.

The following week was the most frustrating of Talon's life and that was saying a lot, considering how old he was.

There were simply no clues to follow.

The witches assured them they'd double-checked every time a demon portaled in and out, to make sure the portals were closed. Not a single one had been left open.

They also weren't aware of any crossings to other realms and no one knew how to contact Starlight's parents to find out if she'd taken Jasmine to see them.

Then, much to everyone's surprise, a hell-cat sauntered into the vampire coven house as if she belonged there.

"What are you doing in here, little beastie?" Talon asked.

"Mrawr." She circled his legs, rubbing against him and leaving fur behind, he was sure.

He leaned over and rubbed her back and sides firmly, grinning as her purr rumbled through the room.

A moment later, she sauntered back out again.

"Man, you gotta tell me what you did to deserve that," Blade said. "None of those hell-cats will let me near them, let alone pet them. It's like a trap, you know. They're so damn cute and you go up to them, crooning and speaking in baby-talk and just as you're reaching out to pet them, you've got seven-foot claws and fangs of death brushing against your jugular."

Talon let out a snort of laughter. "That's always been my experience too, so I have no idea why she let me pet her this time."

"I bet it's because you're the heir to the throne. Lucky bastard," Blade muttered. "Well, lucky to pet the cats, not lucky to inherit the throne."

"Yeah, no shit."

"Jeez, Talon," Joryn said as he walked into the room. "I know you're upset about Starlight and Jasmine, but if that's toilet paper on your shoe, I'm taking away your Vamp Card."

Talon and Blade both looked down and sure enough, there was something stuck to the bottom of Talon's shoe. "You moron," he muttered as he lifted his foot and grabbed whatever it is. "This is way too big to be toilet paper. It's—" He let out a growl as he read the letter.

"What is it, Talon?"

"*Satan.* That bastard."

"What about him?"

"Here."

Talon shoved the paper into Blade's chest and stormed off. "You tell my father his brother's dead."

"Now, Talon, let's take a moment." Joryn dove in front of him and held his arms wide. "Let's not invade Hell without a plan, okay?"

"What's going on?" Lassiter walked in.

"Here." Blade handed him the note and Lassiter read it out loud.

Dear Satan,

Merry Christmas!

I hope you and Mrs. Claus have a very happy holiday.

This year I only have two wishes.

My first wish is for my mom. She works a lot and is always saying that she needs a vacation.

I heard all about these special hotels called bed and breakfasts, so maybe you could give my mom a relaxing Christmas at a bed and breakfast.

Breakfast in bed! She loves that.

Also, for me, I would really, really, really, really, really love a kitten. I promise to take care of her and love her and make her so very happy.

Please and thank you.

Sincerely,
Jasmine, age 9
Zero, Kansas
xoxoxoxoxoxoxoxo

S TARLIGHT WAS HAPPILY FAMILIARIZING herself with the running of the B&B when a rush of flames in the corner made her yelp.

She leapt to her feet, trying to remember where the fire extinguisher was—did they even *have* fire extinguishers in Hell?—when the flames died away and a man stood there.

She stared at him a moment, trying to remember why he was so familiar and then it hit her. "You're Tempest and Merry's dad."

He was staring at her just as closely. "Interesting that you would remember *that*."

"What?"

He shook his head. "Never mind. It's just that most people know of me as Lucifer, the Prince of Darkness, Lord of the Nine Realms of Hell, and The Beast. Not you, though." He chuckled. "You just refer to me as my daughters' dad."

She shrugged. "Sorry, but Merry showed me a picture of you once. I'm really good with faces."

"Hmm. That could explain it." He stared at her for

a long moment, a perplexed look on his face. "Still, this is a very interesting development."

"What do you mean?"

"As if my life wasn't complicated enough." He sighed. "Well, there's nothing to be done about it now. The fat's in the fire, as they say."

"Um, okay."

"Anyway. None of that has anything to do with why I'm here, which is because I understand that you just took an oath as the new manager of my B&B."

"*Your* B&B? Well, I guess that makes sense, but I didn't take an oath. I just said yes when—"

"When Lekhleth asked you to take over managing the B&B."

"Well, yes."

"Did your parents teach you nothing as they dragged you from realm to realm?"

Starlight winced. "I'm not even going to ask how you know that, but suffice it to say I'm out of practice. This is the first realm I've visited in ten years, so I didn't *mean* to take an oath. Honestly, though, I'm not sorry I did. I love this B&B and so does Jasmine. We feel like we belong here."

"Interesting. You came with Jasmine?"

"You've met my daughter?"

"*You're* Jasmine's mom? The one who loves breakfast in bed?"

"Seriously? Did she show that letter to everyone but me?"

"How old is your daughter?" he demanded.

"She's nine. Why?"

"Right, of course. That's what the letter said. I have to sit down." With that abrupt statement, Lucifer made his way to the couch, where he collapsed, seemingly in shock.

"Is it a problem? That I have a child, I mean?" She hadn't even considered that they might not want a child staying at the B&B long-term. Then again, it's not like anyone official offered her the job. She just accepted because it seemed the perfect fit for them.

"No, no, no. Of course not, no. We've just never had a child living here before." He glanced around, an annoyed look on his face. "And the B&B didn't see fit to inform me of the situation either. No matter, though, so long as she was made to feel welcome."

"Oh, she definitely was."

"Excellent. And have you decided on a school?"

Yeah, that was a problem. "I haven't quite figured that out yet." It was the one hitch that was causing her angst. After all, she'd been a child with no school, her education only achieved through what she learned from her parents as they traveled through the realms. She didn't want that for her daughter. "But she's got another week of holiday left, so I have a bit of time to figure things out."

"Hm. Well, there are a number of schools for demons she can choose from. One's fairly close, in fact."

"Oh, I don't think—"

"A demon school?" Jasmine came rushing into the room, one cat perched on her shoulder, another cat in her arms and three others chasing behind her. "That would be so cool! Can I attend the demon school, Mom? Can I?"

"Uh—"

"Oh, this is just fabulous," Lucifer said, staring at Jasmine, mouth agape. "I knew Talon was an idiot."

"What are you talking about?"

"He *has* met Jasmine, hasn't he?"

Starlight nodded. "Of course, he has."

"Like I said. What an idiot."

Starlight narrowed her eyes at Lucifer, wondering if he was implying what she thought he was. And did that mean Lucifer actually knew what had happened ten years ago? And if so, how was that possible?

She'd never been to the Hell Realm before this

week, though strangely she'd recognized where they were almost immediately. She'd figured it was because along the way she must have seen some pictures or something, but now she had to wonder if she'd been here before.

That made no sense, though. The only place she'd ever lost her memories had been at the Jamesville Shenanigans and while it was connected to a number of Realms, not even one of the Nine Realms of Hell was among them.

"I guess I'm not getting an answer right now, Mistletoe," Jasmine said mournfully as she walked slowly out of the room, dragging her feet and throwing sad faces over her shoulder at Starlight.

Normally Starlight would find her daughter's antics hilarious, but right now she was feeling a bit stressed by the way Lucifer was staring at her daughter like he'd seen a ghost. "I don't understand what's happening right now and I don't like it."

"Eh, it's nothing." He waved a hand dismissively. "You know, I thought raising Tempest and Merry was difficult, but those twins—what were their names again?"

"I don't know any twins."

"No, I don't suppose you do. Or you don't remember them anyway. I doubt they remember you either. The spell they cast that day was quite powerful. Well. Cast is a strong word. It implies intent and that really wasn't the case. After all, they were barely in their teens at the time—such a *volatile* time for humans. You know, half-demon hybrids were definitely a challenge to raise, but full-blooded witches, especially ones as powerful as those two, well, I wouldn't have wanted to be their father, or mother, for that matter."

"I literally have no idea what you're talking about."

"Like I said, that spell was powerful."

"What spell?"

He just grinned at her. "Anyway, I'm rather surprised your mate hasn't shown up yet."

"Probably because I'm human and don't have a mate."

He let out a huge sigh. "You know, that spell is starting to piss me off."

"Satan!" The shout was accompanied by a rush of flames in the center of the room.

"Ah, speak of the—well, not devil, but close enough." Satan smirked.

The flames died down to reveal Talon looking absolutely furious. "How dare you?"

Starlight stared, wondering what had him so riled up.

"You have no right to just come into Zero and steal my—Starlight?" Talon broke off when caught sight of her, then lunged forward and hauled her into his arms, hugging her tight. "I was so worried about you. You just disappeared. No one knew where you were or how to find you."

Starlight was horrified to realize she hadn't thought once about informing anyone back home where they'd gone. "I'm sorry, Talon. I didn't realize anyone would notice."

"Of course I noticed! Now, where's Jasmine?"

"Here I am, Talon." Jasmine ran back into the room, still hauling those same two kittens around—or maybe they were different ones, it was so hard to tell— one in her arms and the other on her shoulder, with three more—no, make that five, following behind.

"Excellent." He quickly scooped Jasmine into his arms, cats and all, threw an arm around Starlight, and in a rush of flames, hauled them out of Hell.

At least, that's what Starlight assumed he was trying to do, but the flames didn't seem to work on her *or* on Jasmine.

Starlight stumbled and barely managed to catch Jasmine in her arms when Talon disappeared.

With yowls of discontent, the two cats leapt free when Jasmine latched her arms and legs around

Starlight, clutching her close, as they stared at the spot where Talon had been standing. "Where'd he go, Mama?"

"I have no idea, baby."

"I gotta check on my kitties."

"All right." Starlight set her down and Jasmine rushed over to the cats, where she settled on the floor, crooning to them and petting them until the whole room echoed with the rumbling purrs of half a dozen hell-cats.

At that moment, Talon reappeared in a rush of flames, along with Lassiter, Blade, Dinara and three other vampires Starlight recognized from the diner, but didn't know their names.

Everyone but Talon made an instant beeline for the buffet in the connected dining room, something Starlight could completely relate to, as the food in this place was divine. Still, she couldn't help but stare, fascinated as always, by the fact that vampires could actually consume food.

"Welcome, everyone!" Lucifer, who was still lounging on the couch, exclaimed, dragging her attention back to him. "It's been a long time since you vampires deigned to visit your home realm."

"What have you done, Lucifer?" Talon growled. "Why is my—Starlight and her child trapped in Hell?"

"Trapped?" Starlight spoke faintly, horrified. Had a simple 'yes' just destroyed her daughter's future? Was Starlight as terrible a parent as hers had been, always putting adventure over the wellbeing of her daughter?

"Oh, don't be so melodramatic," Lucifer said. "They're not trapped, as least not permanently. You see, Starlight accepted the job as manager of the B&B."

"The B&B," Talon repeated slowly. "Are you referring to Hell's Bed & Breakfast?" He glanced around. "*This* Bed & Breakfast?"

"I am, yes."

Talon whirled to face Starlight. "You took an Oath of Service?"

"I, well. Is that what it's called? I mean, I agreed to manage it."

"And did the B&B accept your oath? Has it given you things? Has it made any of your wishes come true?"

"All the time!" Jasmine exclaimed."It made me a playroom and a library for Mom. It also gives me hot chocolate and cookies whenever I want them."

"Oh, great," Starlight muttered. No wonder her daughter was bouncing off the walls all the time. "She's right, but it's been doing that ever since we arrived and I only accepted the position yesterday."

"Unbelievable." Talon glared at Lucifer. "How did

you manipulate the B&B into adopting them so quickly?"

Lucifer snorted. "Look, I know you think I'm all powerful, but even I can't make Hell's B&B do what it doesn't want to. If I could, don't you think I would have gotten it to adopt Merry instead?"

"I don't know. Would you have? Merry's now in the earth realm, taken in by her mate's wolf pack and I guarantee she's a lot happier than she was running this B&B. You can't tell me you didn't mean for that to happen."

"Again, you assign me more power than I really have, *especially* if you think I can control the actions of either one of your cousins." Satan shrugged.

"Wait," Starlight said, brain misfiring as she attempted to make sense of the relationships. "You and Merry are cousins? So, that means—"

Talon sighed. "Unfortunately, yes. Starlight, this is my Uncle Lucy. Lucy, my Starlight and her daughter, Jasmine."

Starlight shivered at the introduction, secretly thrilled that Talon kept claiming her as his own.

"How'd you hear that nickname?" Lucy asked. "Which, by the way, I kind of like. Don't tell the wolf. For that matter, how'd you know about Merry and the wolf pack?"

"Merry and I have always gotten along," Talon said. "She texts me regular updates, plus she posted a picture of you standing over her mate and labeled it Sam Meets Uncle Lucy. What the hell did you do to him?"

"She took a picture of me?" Lucy roared. "And posted it on social media? What is wrong with that woman?"

"Eh, it's not like she posted it on Facebook or anything. She just pinned it to the Shenanigans board. You should be thrilled. It's gotten somewhere around 7 million likes and 2 million comments."

"That's even worse!"

Talon grinned. "Is it?"

"I have no idea what's going on right now," Starlight said, setting her hands on her hips, "but you two are starting to freak me out."

"Eh, just ignore those two, Starlight," Lassiter called from the dining room. "Come join us for some breakfast. Jasmine, you hungry?"

"Sure!" Jasmine bounced up from where she was playing with the kittens by the fireplace and ran into the dining room to join the vampires, who immediately started building her a plate, each vampire trying to find her the "best of the best" for breakfast.

"The cinnamon rolls are the best," Jasmine informed them.

"Are they now?" Blade asked. "Personally, I think the bear claws are the best."

"No way. Besides, Mama says no one makes bear claws quite like the bears in the Ice Realm. She says these are a poor substitute."

Lassiter let out a bark of laughter. "I have no doubt your mama's right. Come along now. Let's do some taste testing." He led Jasmine back to the table and settled her at his side.

Starlight's heart melted a little, watching the vampires work hard to entertain her daughter and make her laugh. They'd always been like that, from the moment they met Jasmine the first day she ran into the diner after school.

And though he was currently occupied, arguing with his uncle, Talon had always been the best of all of them, when it came to Jasmine. He'd been the first to win her affections and was always the first one she went to when she had something to share about her day.

All the paranormals in Zero, Kansas, had accepted Jasmine, despite her being human, and treated her as one of them. Remembering this made Starlight a little homesick, not necessarily for the town, but definitely for the people they'd left behind there.

"Come on, sweetheart." Talon stepped up to sling an arm around her shoulders. "We should probably catch up."

"Finished arguing with your uncle?" She glanced over at the couch, only to realize Lucy was no longer there.

"Eh, something came up, but he'll be back. Like a bad penny."

BYGUL DIDN'T KNOW WHETHER THIS WAS A good development or not, especially now that he realized who the players were.

He couldn't believe he'd forgotten all about those two and their doomed match.

It was that stupid spell. It shouldn't have worked on him at all.

He was a matchmaking cat of the goddesses, for goddess' sake!

He was Freyja's own right-hand cat.

And that *Satan* had actually figured it all out before him was just insulting. That bastard had probably insisted the spell not trap him in its weave in the first place.

Which *clearly* was cheating!

"What's wrong, Bygul?" Soraya asked.

"Everything," he said morosely. Was history about to repeat itself? Had he made a terrible mistake in agreeing to Soraya's demand that they help the human?

If only he'd remembered her sooner. This was a nightmare!

"So your parents are travelers," Talon said as Starlight led him into the library, her favorite room in the house.

"Where'd you hear that?"

"When you disappeared, Dinara investigated, found out who you parents really were. None of us had any idea. No wonder you never blinked an eye when a wolf shifted in the diner or when those zombie spiders came marching through."

"Well, when you grow up traveling the realms, nothing really surprises you anymore. Though a few things came close, like this situation with the B&B. I forgot one of the cardinal rules of traveling the realms. Watch your words."

"Do you not *want* to be the manager?"

"Oh, I do very much. I actually love it here. It's like my dream job."

"Seriously? *Why?*"

"Because it's a really beautiful B&B. I get free room and board for me and my daughter. Plus, Jasmine loves it here. The B&B makes sure she has everything she could ever want or need. She has a fantastic time here. The only thing that makes it a little less than perfect is the lack of playmates, though she adores the kittens and treats them like her best friends."

"Uh, you do realize those kittens are hell-cats in disguise. I mean, sure, they're still kittens, but in their hell-cat form, they're huge and they'll just keep getting bigger."

"I know that. I also know they'll defend my daughter with their lives, rip apart anyone who dares to try and hurt her. She's got the best guard-kitties in all the realms who will make sure she's always safe."

Talon grinned. "You are a unique woman, Starlight. Here I've been going slow, figuring you were human, and therefore, would need some time to adjust."

"Adjust to what?"

He stepped forward, slid a hand around her neck, pulled her close and murmured against her lips, "To the fact that you are mine."

Starlight's breath hitched in her throat. Was he saying what she thought he was?

"Sweet mate, I recognized you the moment I walked into that diner the very first time. It was like we'd met before and I'd just been waiting for you to appear in my life once more."

"I felt the same way," she whispered. "I've always felt that way. Like something was missing and when I saw you for the first time, that missing piece was finally made whole."

"Aw, that's so sweet," Soraya exclaimed.

"Yeah," Bygul said glumly. "Let's hope it doesn't end the same way as last time."

"Last time?" The other three cats chorused.

Bygul sighed. "You *have* heard about Witchgate, right?"

The other three gasped.

"No!" Muezza exclaimed.

"Yes."

"That was them?" Soraya wailed.

"Unfortunately, yes."

"Hold on a minute," Tivali said. "I thought everyone involved had their memories erased, so that the two wouldn't accidentally stumble upon the truth, so how do you know it's them?"

"I'm the matchmaking cat of a goddess," Bygul snapped. "That's how I know."

The other cats just stared at him.

He let out a growl of annoyance. "Fine. I've always had some memories of the event, just not who was involved until now."

"What made you remember?" Soraya asked.

"I'm honestly not sure," Bygul said. "It's like the spell started to dissipate when Satan mentioned the twin witches and then it popped entirely when Talon said Starlight's parents were travelers."

"That makes sense," Tivali said. "I mean, twin witches aren't that common and there can't be that many humans out there who traveled the Realms with their parents."

"I still don't get it," Muezza said. "I thought Kalyn was the one working a match in the Underworld."

"He's right," Tivali said. "That *was* Kalyn's match. He took the blame for everything."

"Of course, he did," Bygul said. "It gave him plenty of ammunition to hold over my head for the rest of our lives."

Muezza sighed. "Your brother does get an inordinate amount of pleasure out of torturing you."

"It's rather disturbing actually," Tivali said.

Four

TALON COULDN'T BELIEVE he'd waited so long when Starlight would clearly have been receptive to the idea of a vampire mate all along.

"Sweet Starlight," he murmured, then kissed her, reveling in the way she wrapped her arms around his neck and kissed him back.

Long moments passed, then he pulled back enough to murmur, "Which room is yours?"

"Second floor. It's the suite at the end of the hall."

With barely a thought, he used the flames of Hell to transport them to the suite's living area, and from there to Starlight's room, which he found simply by letting the B&B guide the flames.

"Another myth destroyed," Starlight said.

"What are you talking about?"

"The myth that fire will destroy vampires."

"Yeah, since we were born of Hell, that's an outrageous exaggeration. My guess is some human somewhere saw one of us use the flames to travel and assumed when the flames died and we weren't there anymore, that we'd been consumed by them."

"That makes sense. So how come they worked on me this time?"

"Because I wasn't trying to take you away from the B&B. As long as we stay on the property, we can pretty much go anywhere."

"So I did destroy my daughter's life."

"No. Satan was right when he said it wasn't permanent. It only lasts as long as it takes you to to convince the B&B that you will always return here because it's your home."

"How do I do that?"

"No one knows, but I'm sure you'll figure it out. Now, mate, I know we've only known each other a year, but it feels more like a decade that I've been waiting to make you mine."

Starlight smiled up at him. "Then let's not wait a moment more."

STARLIGHT SQUEALED WHEN TALON LIFTED her in his arms and launched her toward the bed. She landed with a bounce and a laugh as Talon came down on top of her.

He kissed her and all laughter disappeared in a rush of heat and desire.

They rolled across the bed, pulling at each other's clothes, kissing whatever skin they managed to reveal and reveling in the moment.

Heat spiraled higher and higher, until it almost felt as if the flames of Hell themselves had joined their mating.

Finally, they were naked and the feel of Talon pressing against her, slowly sinking deep, was like coming home.

"Talon," she murmured against his collarbone, licking a tiny bead of sweat that had pearled there.

"Starlight," he groaned, sliding his hands beneath her, lifting her against him and settling back on his haunches so she rode his lap. "My love."

He caught her hair in his fist, pulled her head back and captured her lips with his, spearing his tongue deep to duel with hers and sending new waves of heat sliding through her.

She lifted slowly, then sank back down, then did it again and again, reveling in the feel of him slowly rubbing against her deep inside, filling her, then sliding away, then filling her once more.

Everything coiled tighter and tighter, then he slammed her back to the bed, powered forward and everything burst free.

Her vision sheeted white and she cried out as shudders raked through them both, a spiral of ecstasy and infinite pleasure dragging them under.

Long moments later, Starlight came back to herself, only to realize he was still hard inside her, poised and waiting.

"Talon?"

"Starlight," he groaned. "Please."

She tilted her head languidly and caught her breath at the look in his eyes. "Take what you need," she whispered.

"Are you sure?" His eyes swirled with tiny flames, his fangs had dropped, and absolute need had pulled his face taut.

"Positive, my love."

He dropped his face into the curve of her neck and slowly scraped his fangs against the skin there, causing her to shudder in desire. "Please, Talon," she whimpered as she writhed on the sheets, the heat already building again.

"Sweet Starlight," he murmured, then sank his fangs deep.

The sharp pain instantly morphed to pleasure as Talon pulled back slowly, then sank deep, the slow, gliding movements of his cock mirroring the pulse of his fangs as he drank his fill.

She arched and cried out as he hit that perfect spot deep inside, again and again until the world disappeared once more, in endless waves of pleasure.

Starlight woke in Talon's arms, filled with an indescribable feeling of joy, one that felt so right and so familiar, she wondered how she'd never felt it before.

This, right here, was *everything*.

He was hers.

She was his.

And it seemed impossible they'd not found each other before now.

"We haven't met before, right?" She lifted her head to ask.

"You mean before we met at the diner?"

She nodded.

"I'm sure I'd remember if we had. I'd give anything to be Jasmine's father."

Starlight's heart dropped.

She'd known it was ridiculous to hope, but she hadn't been able to help herself. Now that hope was gone. If there was any chance at all, Talon would have claimed it immediately.

"You may not be her birth father, but you're the only father figure she's ever known." Starlight sat up so she could see the expression on his face as she continued. "Jasmine loves you. So very much. She has from the first moment she met you."

A look of joy crossed his face. "I love her as well. More than I'd expected, considering some other man gave her to you."

Starlight shrugged. "He matters not. He's never been a part of our lives, but you have, from the moment we met."

"I CAN'T STAND IT!" SORAYA EXCLAIMED. "After all this time, they're reunited at last. It's so romantic."

"It's like the greatest love story ever," Tivali agreed.

"Whatever," Bygul grumbled. "This greatest love

story had a tragic ending a decade ago and I'm not holding my breath it won't happen again."

"It can't have been *that* tragic," Muezza said. "Both are still alive and look, they're back together."

"Of course, it was tragic! Jasmine's been without her father her entire life. How is that not tragic? *Also*, and more importantly, I've had to deal with the guilt ever since. Kalyn just thought it was funny, but then he loves a bit of chaos."

"A lot of chaos," Tivali muttered.

"And the twins! Their mother cracked down hard on them, probably making it even more difficult for them to gain control of their powers. Last I heard, one of the twins had caused a citywide blackout where they live."

"You mean, they never gained control?" Soraya exclaimed.

"Well, it's not like I'm keeping tabs on them. I did check back in when they reached the age of majority for witches, but as far as I could tell, nothing had really changed at that point. That's been a while though."

"So, it's unlikely they could reverse the spell they cast upon Starlight," Tivali said.

"Highly doubtful," Bygul said. "In fact, we can only hope those two don't choose to attempt another mating celebration."

"Oh, but why?" Soraya asked. "After all they've been through, they deserve—"

"Do you want history repeating itself? Do you not understand what happens when the Prince of Demons has a mating celebration? Chaos! That's what happens! Chaos. Everyone wants to attend the celebration of the century and that's how doorways get left open and human witches end up wandering in and setting mate-bonds afire."

"Oh, don't exaggerate," Muezza said. "There were no flames involved."

"How would you know?" Bygul said.

"Because they're witches and this is Hell. The only flames around here are Hell-born and they would never allow witches to command them."

"Okay, fair point," Bygul said. "Even so, the effect was the same. The bond was destroyed."

"Obviously not completely," Tivali said. "After all, look at them!"

"Did they just set the bed on fire?" Soraya exclaimed.

'Well, it is Hell," Bygul said pragmatically.

They spent the day in bed, a time that felt so familiar to Starlight, as if she'd lived this reality a million times before, and was now blessed to be living it again.

Perhaps they'd been mates in another lifetime.

She'd never been one to believe in reincarnation, but the more time she spent with her mate, the more she thought it could be a possibility.

That constant nagging sense of deja vu, as if they'd been there before, done whatever it was already, as if everything was familiar and wonderful and a cherished part of their forgotten history.

Because it would be easy to obsess over the things that nagged that she just couldn't remember, Starlight tried to focus on other things.

Like the answers to a few questions she had.

For example, it turned out that no, there weren't any fire extinguishers in Hell.

But only because they weren't needed since *everything* was fireproof.

She also learned that Hell's B&B was fairly sentient, a fact she'd already figured out for herself, and that it was known for choosing its managers.

"You should be flattered," Talon said. "The B&B's quite picky and has been known to go centuries without a chosen manager, simply because it doesn't deem anyone else worthy."

"I wonder why it didn't choose Lekhleth."

"I don't even know who that is."

"She's a troll Merry convinced to take over so that she could visit Tempest."

"Well, there's your answer right there," Talon said. "If Merry had to convince her, then she wasn't the right person for the job. I take it you took over for this Lekhleth?"

Starlight nodded.

"And did she have to convince you?"

"Of course not. The B&B is wonderful and I can't imagine living anywhere else."

"And there you have it," Talon said. "The B&B would have known you were the right person from the moment you walked in the front door."

Starlight grimaced. "I didn't exactly walk. I woke up here. In this bed, in fact, without a clue as to where we were."

Talon let out a rumbling growl. "I should have known. Satan. He can't be trusted."

"You think Lucifer brought us here?"

"I know he did."

"But *why*?"

Before Talon could respond, a knock came on the door. "Mama!"

Starlight bolted to her feet, threw Talon's jeans at him and started struggling into hers. "Just a moment, darling." She whirled on Talon and hissed, "Get dressed. Quickly."

Talon let out a rumble of laughter, even as he pulled on his jeans and t-shirt.

Frantically finger combing her hair, Starlight walked to the door. A quick glance over her shoulder showed that Talon was dressed again, but the bed behind him was a disaster and told a tale of its own.

She darted back across the room, grabbed the sheets, threw them onto the bed and then tossed the comforter on top.

Talon chuckled, but helped her smooth everything down, then, when she turned away to head back to the door, caught her around the shoulders, pulled her close and kissed her. Setting her back on her feet, he winked at her and said, "There, that's better."

With that, he walked away.

"What's better? Wait, don't open—Talon!"

But it was too late.

He flung open the door and grinned down at Jasmine. "Hey there, munchkin. What have you been up to?"

Jasmine grinned back. "Playing with my kitties." She sauntered inside, said kitties following behind. "Hi Mama. What have *you* two been up to?"

"Just hanging out," Starlight said.

"Hmm." Jasmine narrowed her eyes, glancing back and forth between the two of them. "I suppose that's okay, but you know you're supposed to invite me too, right?"

"Oh, I'm very sorry, Your Highness." Talon gave a sweeping bow. "Allow me to invite you now. Would you like to join us?"

"Well, I don't know. What are you doing? Is it going to be boring, adult stuff or is it going to be fun?"

"While I assure you that nothing your mother and I get up to is boring to us." He winked at Starlight, who blushed in response. "We are open to suggestions. What would you like to do?"

"Play *Monopoly*."

Starlight snorted at the look of horror on Talon's face.

"Right," Talon said. "Aren't there any other games you'd like to play? Surely the B&B has provided some new games that you've never played before."

"Maybe," Jasmine said. "I'll go check. Come along, Noel, Jingles, Holly, Ginger and Mistletoe."

"You named them all?" Starlight asked.

"Yep. Joy and Snow Dancer are napping with their mama." With that, Jasmine darted out of the room and down the hall.

They ended up dragging some of the board games from Jasmine's playroom into the main room of the B&B and playing a cutthroat role-playing game called Hell's Kitties with the vampires *and* Lucifer, who returned in a rush of flames, just like Talon predicted.

When it became clear the game was a bit inappropriate for a nine-year-old, Starlight protested, but Jasmine insisted it was fine and awesome and the best game ever invented. "I just have to stay and play. Please, Mom!"

Feeling like the worst mother ever, Starlight relented, despite the "good guys" of the game being assassin hell-kitties and their charming demon-thief companions.

Their mission was convoluted, involving lands to acquire and hellhounds to target, which made absolutely no sense. When Starlight tried to clarify things— for example, were the hellhounds the owners of these lands, in which case, were the kitties and demons just evil colonizers—everyone scoffed and told her to pipe down with her morals.

So she glared at the board and played a game that

made no sense, building more and more Shenanigans and assassinating poor, defenseless hellhounds.

The game just went on and on and on until she thought she might go crazy with impatience.

"*Why* are we building another Shenanigans?" she finally demanded.

"For safety and security," Jasmine said for what had to be the twentieth time in the last hour.

"But we already have—" Starlight scanned the board. "—fifteen and those are just the ones that *we* built. There can't be room for anything else at this point. Unless we're building a Shenanigans grocery store."

"*Mom*. There's no such thing as a Shenanigans grocery store."

"Well, why not? Don't paranormals deserve to buy food in peace?"

"Whatever."

As far as Starlight was concerned, Hell's Kitties was *worse* than Monopoly and it was so annoying that Talon didn't seem to agree.

On the other hand, it was quite gratifying to watch him and Jasmine work together to decide where they were going to build their next Shenanigans.

"For demon's sake!" Blake exclaimed. "You're pushing us out into marsh territory."

"Get used to it," Jasmine said with an evil cackle. "Talon and I are so close to ruling the nine realms of Hell!"

"What's this now?" Lucifer set his hands on his hips and glared down at Jasmine, who simply collapsed onto the floor in peels of laughter.

It brought joy to Starlight's heart to see everyone in the room smile at the sound of her daughter's laughter.

They might be in the Hell realm, but as far as Starlight was concerned, they were pretty damn close to Heaven.

Five

"AND THAT'S A wrap," Bygul said. "I say we head on back to the earth realm and start matching the rest of the Zero Coven, what do you guys say?"

"What?" Soraya exclaimed. "But they haven't remembered that they're mates."

"They don't have to remember," Bygul said. "They *know* they're mates. They just mated."

"Maybe so," Tivali said, "but Talon still has no idea he's Jasmine's father. We have to make that right."

Bygul groaned. "And how exactly are we going to do that?"

"I have an idea," Soraya said.

"Do I want to hear it?" Bygul asked.

"Probably not."

"MAMA, ARE YOU AND TALON GONNA GET married?"

Starlight froze in the act of pulling the covers over Jasmine, then continued to tuck her in, before sitting down beside her. "I don't know, sweetheart. He hasn't asked me and marriage is more of a human thing than a paranormal one."

"That's true. So, are you mates then?"

Starlight hesitated, then nodded. "Yes, darling, we are. How do you feel about that?"

"I think it's great. If you get married, then Talon will be my dad, right?"

"That's right. Would you like that?"

Jasmine nodded. "Can we do that soon?"

"Well, it's not just our decision, you know. Talon has to want to get married, but no matter what happens, I know for a fact that he loves you like you're his very own and that will never change."

"I know that, Mama, but I want us to be a family."

Starlight nodded.

The sound of a throat clearing had them both glancing at the door, where Talon stood, hands in his jeans pockets, watching them with so much tenderness and love that tears stung Starlight's eyes.

"Jasmine," Talon said solemnly, "it would be my greatest honor to be your father and to be your mother's husband. I want nothing more than for the three of us to be a family."

Jasmine's face lit up and she launched herself from the bed in one swift move.

Talon leapt forward and caught her in his arms, hugging her tight.

"When?" Jasmine demanded. "When can we have a mating celebration? That's what paranormals have, right? Not a wedding, but a mating celebration."

"That's right. We can have one as soon as you'd like."

"Tomorrow?"

He chuckled. "Maybe not tomorrow, but I bet we can make it happen by this Saturday."

"That's five whole days away."

He grinned. "I know, but that gives us time to track down your grandparents and invite them. Is that okay?"

She let out a huge sigh, but then nodded. "I suppose it'll have to do." She leaned in and kissed his cheek, then said, "You can put me down now."

"Got it." He walked over to the bed and set her back down, then pulled the covers over her.

She scowled at them both. "Seriously? You expect me to sleep now? After such an amazing decision was just made?"

Starlight burst into laughter, then leaned over and smothered Jasmine's face in kisses. "You, baby, are the light of my life. Never change. I love you so much."

"I love you too, Mama, but this bedtime BS isn't right."

Starlight let out a snort, then struggled to tamp down on her hilarity before pulling back to pin her daughter with a stern look, or as stern a look as she could manage in the circumstances, given how incredibly happy she was in that moment. "Bedtime. Tomorrow is soon enough to start making plans."

Jasmine let out a huff, then called out, "Well, come on, then. We're not getting a reprieve after all. Time to sleep!"

As if they'd all just been waiting for the word, cats came from every direction, launching for the bed.

Talon and Starlight both jerked back and leapt to their feet, then watched as one mama cat and seven kittens landed on the bed, walked in circles and eventually settled down so that they completely surrounded Jasmine on all sides.

"Good night, darling," Starlight murmured, walking to the door with Talon.

"Night, Mom. Night, Talon."

"Good night, sweet Jasmine." Talon closed the door behind them, then turned and pulled Starlight into his arms. "You both just made all my dreams come true." He kissed her, then lifted her into his arms and carried her down the hall into her bedroom—*their* bedroom now—where he proceeded to rock her world once more.

The next five days were a whirlwind of activity.

Starlight had no idea if the messages she sent her parents would get to them in time, but she did what she could, reaching out in every way they'd ever communicated to each other over the years, then turned her attention to other priorities.

Namely, the Bed & Breakfast, which had gotten a little testy lately.

It seemed to be trying to send her a message, but she had no idea what that message was.

It'd be nice if the visitors it kept drawing in would just *tell* her the message, but apparently that would be too easy.

Instead, visitors just kept arriving, one after the other, most of them from thin air.

The first one walked through the wall in the dining

room, startling Starlight and the guests eating there at the time.

He introduced himself as Gregor, manager of the only Hotel Shenanigans in all of Hell.

"Really?" Starlight said, a strange feeling washing over her, as if she'd met Gregor before or perhaps been to his hotel, which was quite simply impossible, since this was actually the first time she'd ever visited the Hell realm and she'd not been able to leave the B&B since arriving. "I don't think I've been there before."

"Well, the hotel's in the first realm of Hell, which is quite a ways from here. Still, you should visit us sometime." He glanced around. "I've heard so much about Hell's B&B through the years, but never really had a chance to visit. It's interesting the hotel sent me here now."

"Did it?"

"It did indeed. It's been quite some time since I've been called to serve in this way."

"I'm sorry. I'm afraid I don't understand."

"Oh, don't worry about it. I imagine I'll just be here for the day. Just relax. It was very nice to meet you." With that, he wandered off.

Throughout the day, she caught glimpses of him chatting with various guests, stroking the hell-kitties and getting a tour of the B&B from Jasmine.

Normally, Starlight would never be okay with her daughter spending so much time with a stranger, but with hell-kitties hounding her footsteps and the B&B itself so fond of her, Starlight wasn't worried at all.

Eventually, Jasmine came bounding back, hell-kittens in her wake, to inform Starlight that Gregor had enjoyed the tour and had bowed over her hand before wishing her well and disappearing through the wall in the library.

"Isn't that amazing, Mom?"

"It really is. I have no explanation, but it really is."

The next several days saw a slew of visitors from Shenanigan hotels and B&Bs all over the realms. Many of the visitors Starlight had met before, having stayed in their establishments throughout her travels, and they were absolutely thrilled to discover she was the new manager of Hell's B&B.

By the day before their mating ceremony, Starlight was utterly exhausted from the constant round of visitors and she was blaming the B&B.

Hands on hips, she stood in the middle of her quarters and glared around her. "What in all the realms is going on? You do realize I have a mating celebration in less than twenty-four hours, right?

"Don't get me wrong. I really do appreciate seeing so many people that I've met through my travels and I absolutely love hearing their stories of what it's like to run a Shenanigans B&B or a Shenanigans hotel, but I have to concentrate on my daughter and our last night together before the mating celebration.

"Perhaps you can tone down the visits until next week sometime?"

And now she'd gone officially mad, talking to a building, as if it might actually respond.

Of course, it didn't.

Then again, no other visitors arrived for the rest of the evening, so perhaps she wasn't crazy after all.

Regardless of whether the lack of visitors was coincidence or not, she was quite grateful, especially since the plans for the mating celebration had gotten completely out of hand.

The quiet, family and friends only celebration she'd hoped for had transformed into something else entirely.

The only saving grace was that the B&B wasn't yet allowing Starlight or Jasmine to travel off its grounds, which meant the celebration couldn't take place at Lucifer's compound in the third realm of Hell, as he'd initially demanded.

Instead, it would take place at the B&B itself, which was great news as far as Starlight was concerned.

It was a small, quiet venue and would by necessity, limit the number of paranormals they could invite.

Then, she discovered the B&B apparently had acres and acres of land surrounding it, and to her horror, the vampires were planning a huge, *outside* celebration.

"IT'S MY WORST NIGHTMARE," BYGUL SAID. "Has Satan learned nothing from the past?"

"Oh, come on, what's the worst that could happen?"

"Soraya!" Bygul, Muezza and Tivali all shouted at once.

"What? I'm just saying—"

"Stop, for goddess' sake!" Tivali exclaimed. "You'll tempt the fates."

THE MORNING OF THEIR MATING CELEBRATION dawned bright and early.

Bright because every morning, afternoon, evening *and* night was bright in Hell.

Due to all the flames.

Early because there was so much to do.

Starlight's parents had arrived in a rush the night before, delighting Jasmine and truthfully, Starlight as well.

She'd introduced them to Talon and his family, and they'd all spent the evening together, laughing and talking.

It wasn't quite the evening she'd planned, with just the two of them, Starlight and Jasmine, but it was perfect nonetheless.

She woke the next morning, still filled with that joy of a perfect evening and that feeling of a perfect life, having slipped through her fingers once, now right there, about to start.

It was when she looked outside, though, and saw what waited, what had to be endured before she could finally experience that perfect life, that reality cracked the perfection, just a little.

Somehow, overnight, the flames surrounding the B&B had been driven back and now there was a huge dance floor, long party tents filled with tables and chairs, food trucks, a giant bounce castle (for goddess' sake!), a maze and a Ferris wheel. And that was just what she could see from her bedroom window.

Dragging in a deep breath, Starlight decided not to even think about it. If she didn't think about it, it didn't exist and that was that.

It was just a small, intimate, mating celebration, nothing too huge, nothing too elaborate, just her and Talon and their families.

And every other demon in all the realms who wanted to celebrate the mating of their prince.

No, no, no.

Just her.

Just Jasmine.

Just Talon.

Their families.

No one else.

Just rulers and influential leaders of the other realms, since her mate was something of a political figure, being the freaking Prince of Demons.

But no.

Just her.

Jasmine.

Talon.

Their families.

That's all.

"Mom, are you okay?"

"Uh-huh."

"Why are you sitting in the closet?"

Starlight looked up.

Huh.

This was new.

She'd never been one to hide in closets before, but apparently the thought of huge crowds at her mating ceremony turned her into a sniveling coward.

Dragging in a deep breath, Starlight smiled at her daughter. "Just taking a moment. You know, before we're surrounded by people all day."

Jasmine walked over and plopped down beside her. "You're nervous, aren't you?"

Starlight chuckled and wrapped an arm around her daughter's shoulders, pulled her close and kissed the top of her head. "Terribly. I didn't know I would be, but now I am."

"It's going to be okay. I know it is. This is the best thing that could have ever happened to us, Mama."

"You think?"

Jasmine nodded. "I've been waiting forever. It was taking way too long."

Starlight pulled back to see Jasmine's face. "What do you mean? What was taking too long?"

"You and Talon getting together."

Starlight raised an eyebrow.

"You thought we should be together, huh?"

"Mom, it was totally obvious from the very beginning."

"What was?"

"That you two were mates."

Starlight thought about that a moment and about Talon's conviction that Satan was the reason they'd both arrived here in Hell.

"Jasmine, do you know who brought us to Hell?"

"Uncle Lucy did, of course."

"Uncle Lucy?"

"He said I could call him that, on account of him being Talon's uncle and Talon's gonna be my dad."

Starlight had to think about that for a moment. "When did you and *Lucy* talk about this?"

Jasmine shrugged. "I don't know."

"Did *Lucy* tell you he brought us here?"

"No, but it's kind of obvious, isn't it?"

"I don't know. Is it?"

"Well, he got my letter, didn't he?"

"Your letter to Santa?"

"Uh-huh."

"Why would Lucifer end up with your letter to Santa?"

"Because I misspelled Santa, of course."

So many thoughts swirled in Starlight's head at that moment, she didn't even know how to sort them out.

One thought soared to the top, though.

Jasmine was a truly exceptional child. Smart, an incredible writer and the top speller in her class. There was *no way* she didn't know how to spell Santa.

"Why would you address your letter to Satan instead of to Santa, Jasmine?"

Jasmine shrugged. "I don't know. It just seemed like the right thing to do."

"Did it?"

"Uh-huh."

"Well, I don't know why you did it, but since it brought us to the B&B and set us on our new life path, I'm pretty happy you did."

Jasmine beamed up at her. "Me too, Mama. Are you ready to go celebrate now?"

"I'm ready."

"I CAN'T BELIEVE you were flirting with that angel, Harry!" Lily hovered mid-air, wings beating furiously, arms crossed, glaring at him.

"I wasn't flirting with her, you crazy fairy. I was checking her in."

"Well, *she* was checking you *out*."

Harry grinned. "Now that's not my fault. What would you have me do? Put a bag over my head?"

"If it would help, yes!"

He chuckled. "Are you being serious right now? Because I have to go check a room on the fifth floor." He walked to the elevator, pushed the button, then stepped inside when the doors opened. He turned and grinned at his mate. "You coming?"

She scowled at him for a moment, then, as the doors started to close, zipped forward and into the elevator with him.

He pushed the button for the fifth floor, then turned to face his mate, a wicked grin on his face. He was about to continue teasing her, when the elevator dropped, causing them both to yelp.

Lily leapt for him and wrapped herself around him. "Why is the elevator going down, Harry? What button did you push?"

"The fifth floor, of course."

"You didn't push the second and third buttons together?" she asked suspiciously.

"You know I don't do that. Even when I *want* to go there, I don't push those buttons together. Besides, the elevator's only ever gone up before."

"Then why are we going down?"

"How the hell should I know? This elevator has a mind of its own, you know that."

"There's no basement in this hotel," Lily snapped. "Therefore, logically, we should not be going down."

"Are you seriously trying to apply logic to a Hotel Shenanigans?" Harry demanded.

She scowled. "I'm just saying we've never gone down before and this is a long, long, long way down. Why hasn't it stopped yet?"

"Not a clue," Harry said cheerfully.

"And where is it sending us?"

"Guess we'll find out whenever we get there."

"Do we seriously have to go to this mating celebration?" Serena demanded. "You know I hate these things."

Samantha rolled her eyes. "Look, I tried to get us out of it, but Mother said we were both required to attend. Apparently, when the Prince of Demons sends out an invitation, *everyone* attends."

"Whatever. At least Neil agreed to accompany me. Is Jack going with you?"

"Are you kidding? Jack would tie me to the bed before he'd let me leave this realm without him."

Serena snickered. "How are we getting there anyway?"

"Who knows? Mother's got a plan, I'm sure."

"Well, I don't know about you, but I am just full of dread about this trip, which is kind of weird, don't you think? Normally, I'd be thrilled to go on a trip, even one that takes us to the so-called Hell realm.

Usually, I'm the adventurous one. Yet, I'm a ball of anxiety about this trip."

"Well, it is a bit weird that you're feeling that way, but honestly? I am too. Like something tickling at the back of my brain, trying to get me to remember why I should stay away, but I just can't quite put my finger on it."

"That's it exactly!"

"Great. So we're both sure this is a bad idea, yet we're going to go anyway." Samantha scowled. "Why can't we just tell her no for once?"

They stared at each other, then said in unison, "You first."

Samantha sighed glumly. "I guess we're going then."

"I guess so."

HOWEVER CRAZY STARLIGHT HAD EXPECTED things to get, she'd not even hit the tip of the iceberg.

There were people *everywhere*.

She stood next to Talon, meeting demon after demon after emissary from this realm or that after

Shenanigans representative after demon. The list went on and on and on. Name after name. Realm after realm. Until she felt as if her brain might explode from information overload.

In the beginning, she'd made Jasmine stand with them, but then when it became clear the endless lines were not going to recede anytime this century, she'd allowed Jasmine to escape with the admonishment to keep the hell-kittens with her at all times and to stay with the Coven.

She knew the vampires would protect Jasmine with their lives, so she wasn't exactly worried about her getting lost or hurt, but Starlight hated to let Jasmine out of her sight when they were surrounded by so many people she didn't know.

Finally, after hours and hours of shaking hands, introductions and endless, meaningless conversations, the lines dwindled until they could see an end in sight.

"OH, MY GODDESS, NO!"

"What is it, Bygul?" Tivali asked.

"It's them!"

"Who?" The other cats chorused.

"The twins. They're at the celebration with their mother. I thought we agreed *only* to slip the mother an invitation."

"It wouldn't have been believable," Soraya said. "Demon tradition is to invite the entire family. They would never leave adult children off the invitation."

"That may be true, Soraya," Tivali said, "but we agreed not to involve the twins."

"I didn't involve them!"

"You included them on the invitation," Bygul said. "That's involvement enough."

"Yes, but we agreed to invite the mother."

"Because she's quite powerful, which means she can reverse the spell safely, but with the chaos twins along, anything could happen."

"Personally, I'm glad the twins came," Muezza said. "Their mother wasn't able to reverse their spell ten years ago, so chances are the only ones who can reverse it now are the twins themselves."

"Exactly what I was saying!" Soraya exclaimed.

"So you just decided to invite them anyway," Tivali said, "even though we all agreed not to?"

"I didn't invite them. I sent the traditional demon invitation, that's all. I was sure their mother would never even mention it to them. After all, why would she want to risk bringing the twins back to the Hell realm?"

"She doesn't remember what happened, Soraya!" Bygul exclaimed.

"What? She cast the spell upon herself as well?"

"The spell wasn't cast on the people. It was cast on the invitation itself, so that anyone who handled one or entered the celebration using one, would lose their memory of the invitation, the celebration and all the events leading up to it."

"Great," Soraya said. "That would have been important information to have *before* I had the invitation delivered to Elizabeth Covington's home."

Bygul sighed. "Well, it's too late now. They're all at the celebration and there's nothing we can do to stop what's coming. I only hope it doesn't turn out to be history repeating itself."

STARLIGHT HAD JUST FINISHED SHAKING THE hands of a pair of identical twins—Samantha and Serena, she thought their names were—when Jasmine came bounding over. "Come on, then." She slipped between the twins, grabbed their hands and pulled them toward their family tent. "You have to sit with us. It's important."

Starlight raised an eyebrow, wondering why of all the paranormals they'd greeted, Jasmine chose those two to invite to their table.

She glanced at Talon, who shrugged, looking as mystified as she was.

They continued greeting the few people left in line —Elizabeth Covington, the twins' mother, and their mates, Neil Beckett and Jack Saunders.

Then, one final group, two fairies and a human who were thoroughly entertaining because they seemed less inclined to notice they were meeting the Prince of Demons and his mate, and more interested in the arguments they were waging.

"I can't believe you didn't warn me this could happen, Logan." The female fairy hovered, wings beating furiously as she glared at the male fairy.

He snorted in response, then said, "You're ridiculous. Why would I warn you when I had no idea myself? It's never happened before, now has it?"

"Oh, so, I suppose this is the very first time and it just happened to drag Harry and me along?"

"Now, Lily," the human—Harry?—murmured at her side. "Let's calm the crazy, shall we?"

She let out a huge gasp and whirled on him, but then whirled back when Logan answered. "Well, no. Because I came from the fairy realm, all by my lonesome, while you two came on an entirely separate trip, from the earth realm."

Lily let out a sound of annoyance, but Logan ignored her, reached out a hand and caught Starlight's in his. "Hello, I'm Logan, representing Shenanigans."

"Not just Shenanigans," Lily interjected. "I'm Lily and we run *Hotel* Shenanigans in the fairy realm."

"I remember you both," Starlight said. "My parents and I stayed in your hotel once. Well, my parents did anyway. I stayed on the earth side."

"Really?" The human asked. "When was this? I'm Harry, by the way. I run the earth side hotel."

"About ten years ago, I think. Maybe a bit more."

"That's impossible," Harry said. "The hotel was closed down at that time."

"Eh, sometimes the leprechauns would come over and run scams on the earth side," Logan said. "They'd open the bar, serve drinks at a ridiculous mark-up and sell hotel rooms that they didn't really own the rights to. It was their way of getting back at the fairies for banning them from the fairy mall."

"They're not banned anymore though," Lily interjected.

"Why would running the bar and renting hotel rooms on the earth side be revenge against the fairies?" Starlight asked.

"Because if the guests were buying drinks and staying in earth side hotel rooms, they *weren't* doing the same on the fairy side." Logan said. "Money from our pockets."

"Straight into theirs." Lily scowled. "Tricky little bastards."

LUC CONSIDERED THIS ENTIRE MATING celebration to be one giant miracle.

It was also terrifyingly similar to the one from a decade before.

So much was different, of course.

The previous ceremony was outrageously formal, while this one had a potluck/carnival sort of feel to it.

Still, the essence of it was the same.

His nephew, Talon, thoroughly enamored with his mate, Starlight, both of them so completely in love, leaning into each other, finding refuge together.

Except this time, there was a little girl, his grandniece, Jasmine, who looked at him with wise eyes that seemed to understand and see entirely too much.

Luc had the sense every time they spoke that Jasmine knew what he'd done and wasn't ever going to forgive him for it.

Therefore, when Jasmine came toward him, towing the witchy twins behind her, Luc was horrified.

How in all the realms had the chaos twins gotten into the celebration at all, let alone been tracked down by Jasmine?

This was some epic, next-level, fate bullshit coming at him right there.

"This is my Uncle Lucy," Jasmine announced when she reached the table where Luc was sitting with his brother, Lassiter, who for once, was being civil and not glaring at the world. "And this is my grand-pop, Lassiter."

Lassiter looked startled, making Luc chuckle.

"This is Samantha." Jasmine pulled out a chair and gestured for Samantha to sit down.

With a bemused look on her face, Samantha did as she was told.

"And this is Serena." Jasmine repeated her gestures with a new chair and Serena also sat down.

"Ladies," Luc said quietly. "Nice to meet you."

"You too," Samantha said.

Serena just nodded.

"It's time to fix things, Uncle Lucy," Jasmine said, a note of steel in her voice he'd never heard from her before.

"You do understand there's a risk of history repeating itself, don't you?"

"I don't care. They need to know. You've gotta take it back, Uncle Lucy. Make it right."

He threw back his head, let out a giant sigh, then said, "Fine. I'll need their mother. And Lassiter, we need the coven. Everyone who's here anyway."

His brother stared at him for a long moment, then said, "So you're finally going to reverse whatever it is you did all those years ago?"

"Whatever I did," Luc said wearily, "I did so at your request and with your permission."

Lassiter stared at him another moment, then nodded and stood. "Very well, brother. I'll gather the Coven."

"IT'S VERY NICE TO SEE YOU AGAIN,

Starlight," Logan said, "but I'm not here representing the hotel."

"What?" Lily exclaimed.

Logan ignored her. "I'm here representing the entire organization of Shenanigans, but specifically those that offer lodging. Hotels, motels, B&Bs, that sort of thing."

"Okay." Starlight wasn't sure what he was getting at.

"You've had a number of Shenanigans visitors lately. They've all taken some time to chat with your employees, your guests, even your daughter, and every last one had nothing but positive things to say."

"Oh, well. Thank you."

Logan opened a folder, pulled out a piece of paper and handed it to Starlight. "Congratulations."

Starlight stared down at the certificate in her hand. It said, "Shenanigans Hotel and Lodging Association, SHLA, formally recognizes Hell's Bed & Breakfast as a Shenanigans Institution, and Starlight Travella, as its Certified Shenanigans Manager. May any paranormal in need find refuge and safety within the walls of this B&B."

Starlight blinked rapidly, attempting to keep the tears from falling.

She hadn't even known this was a possibility. She'd

never have dreamed such a beautiful dream because she couldn't have possibly imagined such an outcome.

She drew in a deep breath and looked up.

Logan smiled at her.

"Thank you," she whispered.

He nodded. "Congratulations again, Starlight. You're the very first manager of a Shenanigans Bed & Breakfast in Hell." He tilted his head and jerked his chin up toward the B&B behind them.

Starlight slowly turned and stared.

The sign in their front yard was bigger than before, with the Shenanigans logo scrawled beneath the words, "Welcome to Hell's B&B."

"Look, Mama!" Jasmine came racing back to her side, kittens as usual bounding in her wake. "Can you believe it? We're a Shenanigans now!"

"I know, baby. It's amazing."

THE HOURS THAT FOLLOWED WERE A TRUE celebration, as they were not only celebrating their mating, but also the transformation of Hell's B&B, as it slid beneath the Shenanigans umbrella.

Of course, everyone in attendance felt compelled to stop by and offer congratulations again, turning their meal into another receiving line as word spread about the new Shenanigans logo.

"It's such an impressive accomplishment," Lucifer kept saying. "I never would have expected it of this place."

Everyone, demons and non-demons alike, seemed to agree.

"I can't wait to see how the B&B changes over time," Blade said.

"It's already changed an awful lot," Jasmine said.

"True," Starlight agreed. "Since we moved here, it's gone through a transformation practically every night."

Jasmine giggled, then asked Starlight to dance.

Since she was thrilled to escape the endless receiving lines, Starlight leapt up, held her hand out to Jasmine and together, they ran onto the dance floor, hand-in-hand.

Of course, people offered their congratulations while they were dancing as well, but the energetic movement kept those conversations to a minimum, just a shouted congrats as people whirled by.

Eventually, Talon joined them and Starlight fell head over heels again, watching him dance Jasmine all around the dance floor, both of their faces incandescent with joy.

When they ran out of energy, they joined the lines at the Ferris wheel and went spinning into the night sky, with Starlight and Talon sneaking kisses over Jasmine's head and making her groan and giggle at the same time.

From the Ferris wheel, they went to the maze, Jasmine and Starlight running ahead, then getting lost and needing rescue by Talon.

Eventually, they made their way through carnival game after carnival game before finally heading back to their tent for dessert.

When they arrived, Starlight was startled to see the tent was packed full of pretty much every vampire she'd ever met and many she hadn't.

"Interesting," Talon murmured. "I wonder what my father's planning."

"Who cares?" Starlight asked. "I heard there was chocolate mousse."

Talon let out a bark of laughter, then said, "Go have a seat, darling, I'll find you your mousse."

A few moments later, Talon was good as his word and delivered the most delicious-looking bowl of mousse she'd ever seen.

She was about to take her first bite when Jasmine announced, "It's time."

Starlight looked up, startled, to see Jasmine standing in the middle of the tent, hands on hips, glaring around at, well, everyone, it seemed.

"Time for what, baby?" Starlight gave her mousse a mournful look before walking over to Jasmine.

"They did something bad and now they need to fix it."

"Who are you talking about?"

"Everyone!"

Starlight chuckled. "Okay, but can you narrow that down a little for me?"

She let out a huge sigh. "Uncle Lucy, the twins, their mama, probably other people too, but them to start."

"It wasn't bad at the time, Jasmine." Lucifer stood and walked toward them. "In fact, it was desperately needed and was our only choice at the time."

"What did you do, Lucy?" Talon asked as he joined them.

He sighed. "Look, it was something you asked me to do." He looked around the tent at all the vampires assembled. "All of you requested this. The one most affected though has requested we attempt to undo what was done." He turned to Jasmine. "As promised,

I will do my best, but none of us can know what will happen next."

Jasmine just crossed her arms and glared at him. "Just fix it."

He nodded, then disappeared in a rush of flames.

A couple seconds later, he reappeared with a frame in his hands. He turned and walked toward where the witches were seated. "Elizabeth, would you do me the supreme favor of attempting to remove the spell cast upon this invitation." He passed the frame to her.

Silence fell as Elizabeth stared down at the frame, an arrested look on her face.

She glanced up at Lucifer, who nodded.

Pushing back her chair, Elizabeth stood, turned the frame over and carefully extracted the paper inside it.

Seven

"IT'S HAPPENING," SORAYA whispered.

The cats watched as Elizabeth Covington slowly picked her way through the spell she'd cast a decade before.

Her fingers plucked at the bits of magic clinging to the invitation and slowly began unraveling the entire thing, tiny sparks flaring and dying as she worked.

What seemed a lifetime later, her eyes flew open and she stared at Lucifer. "Are you certain about this?"

He glanced at Jasmine, who nodded resolutely. "Absolutely."

"Please let this work," Bygul whispered. "Please."

Starlight wasn't sure exactly what was happening.

All she knew was that Jasmine was adamant something had to be fixed and it involved both Lucifer and the witch named Elizabeth Covington.

The look on the witch's face as she stared down at the frame Lucifer had given her made Starlight incredibly curious as to what the invitation inside it said.

Then, she was too busy watching the witch work her magic, to wonder anymore.

There were tiny sparks that flickered and died, over and over again, as Elizabeth plucked at nothing but air, the invitation hovering in front of her.

Finally, it seemed she was done manipulating the air, and opening her eyes, asked Lucifer, "Are you certain about this?"

When Lucifer looked toward Jasmine for assurance, Starlight wrapped an arm around her daughter from behind, pulling her closer, trying as best as she could to reassure her, hating that she didn't understand what was going on with her own daughter.

Jasmine nodded and Lucifer turned back to Elizabeth and gave his approval.

Spreading her hands, Elizabeth clapped them together right above where the invitation hovered.

The invitation burst into flames, then magic rolled across everyone in the tent as the flames died, leaving nothing behind.

Talon gasped, then fell to his knees.

His father, Lassiter staggered and went down as well.

"Talon!" Starlight gave Jasmine a reassuring squeeze, then fell to her knees beside him. "Are you okay?"

He slowly raised his head and stared at her as if he'd never seen her before. "Starlight." He dragged her into his arms and kissed her, ravenously, desperately. He buried his face into her neck and whispered raggedly, "I missed you so much. Even when I didn't remember, you were a gaping wound in my heart and soul." He jerked back suddenly, then turned and stared up at Jasmine who stood beside them, trembling. "Jasmine, my heart."

Jasmine hurtled herself into his arms, burrowing between them, arms wrapped around his neck. "Daddy."

Starlight jerked and stared at them both.

Talon's eyes were closed as he held Jasmine close, tenderness in every line of his body as he lay his head down on hers and wrapped her in his arms. "My precious daughter," he whispered, tears trickling down his face.

Starlight was beginning to feel a little panicked, as if something had happened that she'd been left out of, as if everyone, even her own daughter, understood something she did not, as if her entire identity was a mystery, even to herself.

Lassiter was suddenly there, kneeling beside them, wrapping one arm around his son and the other around Starlight.

"Talon," Lassiter spoke quietly. "Starlight needs you. She needs you both."

"THIS IS TERRIBLE," SAMANTHA WHISPERED, her head throbbing and her heart hurting even more.

"I can't believe we—" Serena looked as stricken as Samantha felt, tears swimming in her eyes.

"What is it, Samantha?" Jack wrapped an arm

around her, no doubt desperate to protect her from something no one could protect her from.

Elizabeth sighed, looking defeated for the first time in Samantha's memory. "Listen, girls. I'm so sorry I couldn't protect you from this."

"You *did* protect us though," Samantha said. "For ten years, your spell protected us from the truth. That's what you were doing, right? Unraveling your own spell."

Elizabeth nodded. "I didn't remember it at the time. The spell I cast removed even my own memories. It had to be done though."

"I don't understand," Serena said. "Was our spell truly that powerful?"

"We were only twelve!" Samantha exclaimed.

"Okay, someone needs to explain what the hell is going on," Neil said.

"Ten years ago, we were all right here, attending this same celebration," Samantha said.

"Mother told us we had to remain behind, but we were curious," Serena said. "We'd never been to the Hell realm before."

"So we followed and had a grand time, exploring and spying and just enjoying ourselves."

"But then, we got caught," Serena whispered.

"One of Mother's witches caught us sneaking slices of cake and so we cast a spell."

"Not even really thinking about it," Samantha said. "We just did it instinctively and then it was too late."

"What kind of spell?" Jack asked.

"A memory spell," Serena said. "It was supposed to just make the woman forget she'd seen us, but as usual, we lost control of our magic and it wiped out a whole lot more."

"Since Starlight and her parents were human," Elizabeth said, "they were especially susceptible to the twins' spell. In the end, Starlight was left with no memories of Talon or their love for each other.

"From that point on, every time she saw Talon, her brain tried to make those connections and remember, but then the spell would reactivate, causing her unspeakable pain," Elizabeth said. "In the end, all Talon could do was let her go, but then he was going mad without his mate, so I cast a secondary spell to help the Vampire Coven forget Starlight entirely."

"You couldn't just undo the twins' spell?" Neil asked.

"Memories are tricky," Elizabeth said. "Trying to undo someone else's memory spell could result in worse damage than if we'd just left it alone. And we couldn't risk Samantha and Serena attempting to reverse it themselves. They were simply too young to have any control of their powers."

"Did you know that about memory spells?" Tivali demanded.

"I didn't," Bygul said.

"So, the *only* ones who can ever reverse that spell," Soraya began.

"Are the chaos twins themselves," Bygul finished.

"This is not good news," Muezza said.

"Not at all," Bygul said. "I'm starting to think you were right, Muezza."

"About what?"

"This match is doomed."

"That's why you've always resisted your magic," Jack said to Samantha. "Some part of you must have remembered and internalized that trauma." He pulled her close and murmured softly in her ear, "I'm so sorry, my love, but you were twelve. A child witch with no control of her magic. Today, you and Serena are powerful witches and if anyone can undo that spell, it's the two of you."

Samantha drew in a deep breath, nodded, then straightened in her chair. "You're right." She kissed him quickly, then turned to her sister. "Come along, Serena. We did great harm ten years ago and it's time to make things right."

Serena stood and followed Samantha toward where the Prince of Demons held his mate, Starlight, and their child, Jasmine, in his arms.

"It's going to be all right, Starlight," the Prince was saying quietly when they arrived.

"Why don't I remember what everyone else does? Why does even Jasmine understand what I do not?"

Samantha and Serena both settled on the ground, on either side of the mated couple.

"It was our fault," Samantha said quietly. "We didn't do it on purpose, but ten years ago, a spell we cast removed your memories, Starlight."

"If you would allow us to try," Serena said, "We will do our best to unravel our spell and return your memories."

Starlight sat back and looked from Samantha to Serena, who nodded in encouragement. "We can help. I promise."

The Demon Prince glared at them. "Are you in control of your magic now or is it still a seething cauldron of chaos?"

"We're in control," Serena assured him. "We won't let you down."

"We promise," Samantha said.

When the Prince nodded, they both reached out and grasped Starlight's hands in theirs.

"Just relax," Samantha said. She reached into the well she shared with her sister and tapped into their power, letting it pour through her, then releasing it back into the well.

She did this several times, sensing Serena doing the same.

When they were ready, they reached out together with their magic and tracked the spell they had once cast.

"It's everywhere, sister," Samantha murmured.

"In her heart, in her bloodstream, in her very cells."

Their eyes flew open.

"What is it?" Talon growled.

"We cannot extract the spell without killing her," Samantha said.

"Unbelievable," Bygul growled. "Who knew a couple twelve-year-old twins could cast such a powerful spell? This is a nightmare."

"It's going to happen again, isn't it?" Soraya wailed. "They're going to have to take away their memories because she still doesn't remember."

"Oh, don't be ridiculous," Tivali said. "The only reason everyone's memories were wiped was because Starlight couldn't even see Talon without crying out in pain. In order to protect her, they had to send her away, which is why Talon started to go mad and why Lucifer had Elizabeth cast the second spell. But look at Starlight now. Sure, she still doesn't remember, but she's been with her mate for the last year and hasn't experienced any pain at all."

"She's right," Muezza said. "It's not exactly the purrfect ending we were all hoping for, but if Starlight has to live without her memories, at least she has her mate with her this time and the Prince of Demons has his mate *and* his daughter."

"Right," Bygul said, struggling to project a bit of

cheer in his voice, but finding it dreadfully difficult. "All's well that ends well, I suppose."

"No!" Jasmine cried out. "You can't kill her!"

"Don't worry," Serena said, trying to understand why her magic kept reaching toward Jasmine. "Is your magic doing what mine is, Samantha?"

"It is. I think it senses Starlight's memories all over her daughter."

"All over *me*?" Jasmine asked.

"She would have been pregnant with you when the spell was cast," Samantha said, "so perhaps that has something to do with it?"

"Well, I have been dreaming about my father all my life. In my dreams, he's dancing with Mom in a grand ballroom, and they're so happy. It's how I knew he'd come back into our lives. I just didn't know when." She threw a glare at her father. "You took long enough."

He chuckled. "I'm so sorry, my sweet Jasmine. Had

I known you were waiting for me, I would have torn apart the realms searching for you.”

“How does Jasmine have my memories when I don’t?” Starlight asked.

“I don’t have them all,” Jasmine protested. “Only a few.”

“Because they’re not yours,” Serena said. “A few might trickle through in your dreams, but most would be inaccessible to you, even though they’re there, just like your mother’s genetics are there and so are your father’s.”

“What I don’t understand is how they survived the memory spell at all,” Samantha said.

“THAT WAS ME!” BYGUL EXCLAIMED excitedly.

“What?” The other cats chorused.

“I was working in the earth realm, checking on an alley cat and her kittens who had just landed on my caseload. Well, I arrived just in time to see two of the earthbound kittens wander through an open portal. Of course, I had to go after them, mostly because I wanted to figure out which idiotic demon left a portal open in the first place."

"Demons," Muezza muttered.

"They're so careless sometimes," Tivali said in disgust.

"Anyway," Bygul continued, "the portal led to the Hell realm, but more specifically, to the mating ceremony of Talon and Starlight. I was surprised to find that Kalyn was also in the building, having followed a witch he'd decided would be a good candidate for one of his matches."

"Oooh, let me guess!" Soraya exclaimed. "It was Elizabeth Covington."

"Exactly. Kalyn always was a moron considering Elizabeth is highly allergic to cats."

Muezza snorted. "Figures."

"Didn't he notice the twins following their mother?" Tivali demanded.

"Of course, he did," Bygul said. "But you know how Kalyn is."

"Chaos is the sweetest of nectars," the others chorused, quoting Kalyn's most ridiculous mantra.

"Well, he got his wish in this case," Bygul said. "He didn't stop the twins, but then, neither did I. He was clear across the ballroom and I was standing next to the cake, trying to coax my kittens from under the table, when the twins cast their spell. I realized what was happening too late. I'd sensed the tiny spark of life deep inside Starlight, so I threw some goddess magic at that little spark to protect it. It was all I could do before the spell took on a life of its own."

"Your goddess magic must have protected her memories," Soraya said in awe.

"That's high level magic, Bygul," Tivali said.

He twitched an ear and said, "Yeah, but she still spent the last decade without her mate."

"We can cast a new spell," Samantha said, excitement rising as she realized what this meant. "One that transfers your memories from Jasmine back to where they belong."

"It won't hurt Jasmine?" Starlight asked.

"Not at all," Samantha said. "She might not get anymore dreams, though."

"That's okay," Jasmine said. "I'd rather my mom have her memories back."

"And it won't hurt Starlight either?" Talon asked.

"It's perfectly safe," Serena said. "A much

simpler spell than the one we cast a decade ago. This one just returns what was lost to its rightful owner."

"Then let's do it," Starlight said. "I'm tired of feeling as if I've lost something precious."

"Ready, sister?" Samantha asked, holding out her left hand.

"Ready," Serena clasped it with her right, then reached for Jasmine's hand while Samantha reached for Starlight's.

Starlight and Jasmine clasped their remaining hands, closing the circle of power between the four of them.

Samantha reached deep into her well, going through the same cycle of power ebbing and flowing as before, then along with her sister, sent their magic cascading over Jasmine, casting the spell slowly, so that it fell over only Starlight's memories, then slowly migrated them from daughter to mother, in a sparkling web of power.

At first, Starlight felt nothing.

Just her daughter's hand in hers and the witch's on the other side.

Then something began to happen.

It felt like tiny sparks were raining down upon her, sparks of power and light.

They settled deep into her bones, into her very marrow, and waited there, sizzling in silence.

For a long moment, nothing happened, then Samantha let go of her hand and the magic inside exploded in a rush of sound and color and swirls of chaos.

Talon's heart pounded as the witches cast a spell over both his mate and daughter.

He had a terrible moment of fear, wondering if he'd done the right thing, then the magic exploded, making both Starlight and Jasmine gasp, backs arching, before falling backward with a ripple of enormous power.

Talon caught Starlight in his arms and his father caught Jasmine in his.

"Starlight?" Talon carefully lowered her to the

floor, aware his father was doing the same thing with Jasmine.

For a long moment, neither responded, then at the same moment, both of their eyes flipped open.

"Talon!" Starlight hurtled herself up and into his arms, clutching him close. "I remember. Oh, Talon, I remember everything." She buried her face in his neck and burst into tears.

For the second time in less than an hour, Talon reached out an arm to his daughter, who threw herself at him, and finally, *finally,* ten years after he first met the mate of his heart and soul, his world was complete.

"I owe you an apology, Luc," Lassiter said quietly.

"You owe me nothing."

"You only did what we asked and we punished you for it."

"I couldn't tell you what I'd done and that would have felt like a betrayal to you. I understand why you left the Hell realm and I don't hold it against you. You couldn't trust me anymore. I can't say I wouldn't have done the same in your place."

Luc felt coated in sadness. Though his nephew finally had his family back, he'd lost ten years with them, and Luc was plagued with the idea that perhaps he hadn't needed to lose them at all.

At least not ten years' worth.

What if they'd tried again? Brought Starlight to Hell every year or so? Might Talon have been reunited with his mate sooner than the ten years he'd waited?

"I know what you're thinking," Lassiter said, "but Talon wasn't willing to take the risk, not when seeing him caused her so much pain over and over again. You had to honor his wishes. That you did so, even knowing we would hate you for it, was a gift we can never repay."

"It was a curse, not a gift," Luc said bitterly.

"It was a gift of time. Time that allowed their love to grow without memories or pain. Time that allowed them to find their way back together again. And now look at them, brother, they're as happy today as they were ten years ago and *you* did that."

Luc watched as his nephew dipped his mate on the dance floor and Jasmine circled around them, joy in every line of her body. Perhaps Lassiter was right. Regardless, there was no use looking to the past.

At that moment, Kyrie jumped into his lap, making him chuckle. "Hello, little beastie. I've missed you, my love." He pet her until her purrs rumbled through the night air, then without looking at Lassiter, admitted, "I've missed you too, brother mine."

STARLIGHT'S HEART WAS SO FULL, SHE FELT AS if she might drown in the joy.

Somewhere deep inside, she was also mourning ten years apart, but for now, for tonight, there was only happiness and joy.

Celebration and homecoming.

A reunion ten years in the making.

Talon spun her out on the dance floor, then spun her back, making her laughter ring out into the night.

"Starlight, congratulations!" Merry whirled by in the arms of a shifter.

"Merry, you came!"

Merry laughed. "I wouldn't miss it for the world! I knew you'd be the perfect manager for the B&B."

"Wait, what?" Starlight spun, but Merry was already out of sight, dancing her way around the dance floor. She had to wait until they spun past again, to say, "You hired Lekhleth to run the B&B, not me."

"She was just the temporary manager until I could figure out how to get you to Hell." She winked at Jasmine. "Good job, partner."

"*Jasmine*?" Talon exclaimed incredulously, staring down at their daughter as if he'd never seen her before.

Jasmine just grinned at him. "You do realize I've known how to spell Santa since I was three years old, right?"

Starlight snickered.

Talon shook his head and chuckled. "Well, would you look at that? Our very own daughter, matchmaker extraordinaire."

"Hey!" Bygul exclaimed. "That's our job, not hers."

"Typical," Muezza muttered.

"I hate when they do that," Soraya said. "They're always giving credit to other humans when clearly it was our efforts as matchmaking cats of the goddesses that gave them their happily ever afters."

"Well, it's not like they can see us," Tivali pointed out. "Besides, the little girl did do her part. After all, she *did* write that letter to Satan."

"And Tempest's familiar delivered it," Soraya said.

"I bet Merry arranged that too," Muezza said.

"I'm starting to realize how much work this particular match required," Bygul said, "and not just from us. It's not unusual to recruit the earthbound cats to help, but hell-kitties, humans, witches, even the devil had his hand to play. I've said it before, but I've never meant it more than today.

"*Great* job, team."

SNOW DANCER RACED BETWEEN THE DANCING feet, chasing his siblings all over the dance floor, never losing sight of his human, Jasmine.

Every once in a while, he darted back to rub against her, shifting sizes as he went.

First, he visited in his housecat size, wrapping around her legs and enjoying the sound of her voice as she bent over to pet him and croon to him, telling him how wonderful he was.

Then, he visited in his hell-cat size, but the smaller one, rubbing against her back, then her front, enjoying the feel of her hands scratching along his spine, then hugging him.

Finally, he shifted to his medium hell-cat size, settling his head on her shoulder and nuzzling her cheek, making her giggle.

"I love you, Snow Dancer." She reached up and scratched him beneath his chin, making him purr and causing her entire body to shake with laughter. "That tickles!"

He gave her one last nuzzle, then darted away to stalk the perimeter of the dance floor, staking out his territory and roaring into the night.

My humans, my B&B, my Jasmine!

His siblings all roared back their agreement. *Ours!*

Wondering about the Chaos Twins?
Read their stories in *Wicked.*

Next up is Lucifer's story in *Valen-Cats.*
Read on for an excerpt.

"This has been a disaster," Tivali lamented, her tail twitching in annoyance.

"A complete nightmare," Bygul growled in agreement. He couldn't believe how poorly things were going with this latest witch.

She was supposed to be the easy one! After all, she'd already found her mate.

"Oh, it's not that bad," Soraya said. "The cats weren't too traumatized and we found each of them homes in the end, didn't we?"

"Not traumatized?" Muezza exclaimed. "That one kitten went completely psycho!"

"I said not *too* traumatized, and that only happened because the vampire tried to pet him,"

Soraya said. "Once we stopped letting the humans see the cats, things got a lot better."

"A lot better?" Tivali exclaimed. "We *still* haven't found a familiar for the garden witch. It's bad enough they keep destroying all her plants."

"It really is a bit of bad luck about her mate," Muezza said.

"We should have anticipated the vampire would be a problem," Bygul said in disgust. "I can't believe it never occurred to me."

"Well, why would it?" Soraya asked. "Hocus Purrcus lets the vampire pet him all the time."

"So does Cookie," Muezza said.

"And the hell-cat wouldn't be bothered if an entire coven of blood-suckers moved in," Tivali said.

"Exactly!" Soraya exclaimed. "Honestly, I think they're more bothered by the wolves."

Bygul licked a paw and rubbed his ear, thinking hard about their next steps. He didn't want to give up, but—

"I think we should take a break," Soraya said. "Not from matchmaking, of course, but from this particular match. We'll find Jo's purrfect familiar soon enough, but in the meantime, I have another rather urgent situation that needs our attention."

"What situation?" Bygul glared at the cat he considered to be more of a liability than an asset in their matchmaking endeavors.

Every time they turned around, Soraya had the most impossible cat she wanted them to match. Either that or she was convinced the most ridiculous humans belonged together. Sure, she sometimes got it right, but just as often, she got it entirely wrong.

Unpredictable.

That's what she was.

"So." Soraya drawled out the word, her whiskers twitching in excitement.

That was *not* a good sign.

Whisker-twitching from Bygul or Tivali usually meant they had a brilliant idea.

Whisker-twitching from Muezza meant he either thought you were an idiot or he was getting ready for some in-depth cleaning.

Whisker-twitching from Soraya, on the other hand, was often a sign of impending disaster.

"I really want to match Jane and I have the purr-fect mate in mind for her."

"Jane," Bygul said. "Who's Jane?"

"The librarian," Muezza and Tivali chorused.

"Again? We already talked about this, Soraya,"

Bygul said. "She's not a witch. We need to finish the witches first. You keep sidetracking us and we'll never get this coven entirely matched."

"I know, but she's witch-adjacent."

Muezza snorted, Tivali's tail started to whip back and forth in agitation and Bygul just stared at Soraya.

When she said nothing else, he finally exploded, "*How* is a non-paranormal human considered witch-adjacent?"

"I thought you'd never ask," she exclaimed excitedly. "It turns out when Merry left Hell to come to Zero, Kansas, she built a tiny doorway between the two realms and one side of that door opens into the library where Jane works."

"*Why* would Merry—you know what? Never mind. I don't want to know." The daughters of Satan were just one of the many reasons Bygul wanted to finish matchmaking this coven and leave Zero, Kansas behind.

"While that's very interesting, Soraya, I'm not sure I understand what that has to do with matching our coven of witches." Bygul was impressed at how patient Tivali sounded when the tip of her tail was whacking the floor in a rapid, repeated pattern that betrayed her annoyance with every beat.

"Well, Merry and Tempest are witches, and Satan's their father, and a couple of Satan's hell-kittens found their way through the doorway, so—"

"What?" Tivali and Muezza shouted the word at the same time Bygul did.

"Anyway, Jane found them, and well, she seems to have decided to adopt them."

"But they're hell-cats!" Bygul exclaimed.

"I don't think she knows that," Soraya said. "They're still young and they haven't shifted to their larger sizes yet."

Bygul groaned. "All right. Fine. We'd better go corral those kittens before Lucifer discovers two of his precious babies have gone missing."

"Oh, it's too late for that," Soraya said. "But it's purrfect, don't you think? Because I'm absolutely positive they're a purrfect match."

"What? Who?" Tivali exclaimed.

"Satan and Jane, of course!"

"Are you insane?" Bygul exploded.

"Sounds more like a match made in Hell," Muezza observed.

"Which makes it pawsitively purrfect for him, don't you think?"

Bygul, Muezza and Tivali just stared at Soraya in

amazement. Because how could a cat—*any* cat, let alone a matchmaking cat of the goddesses—be so completely oblivious?

Start reading *Valen-Cats* today.

Thank you for reading

Satan's Kitty

Please consider leaving a review on your favorite book site.

If you would like to be notified of

Pepper's new releases, please sign up here:

www.peppermcgraw.com/newsletter

Join Pepper's reader groups on Facebook:

Matchmaking Cats of the Goddesses

The Shenanigans Crew

WELCOME TO
HELL'S B&B
A Shenanegans
ESTABLISHMENT

Other Books by Pepper

BLACKTHORN ACADEMY

Monster's Reward

Monster's Madness

MATCHMAKING CATS OF THE GODDESSES

Catnapped

The Real McCat

Unbearably Cute

A Catmas to Remember

This Cat's for You

Santa Kitty

Hocus Purrcus

Abra-CAT-Abra

Tridents & Tails

Her Purrfect Familiar

Chocolate Furnanigans

Satan's Kitty

Valen-Cats

Catanic Rituals

A Beautiful Cat-ship

Going Catty

Grave Cattitude

MURRYSVILLE COALITION

The Crazy Cheetah Lady

One Sad Kitty

SHENANIGANS

Shifter Shenanigans

Witchy Shenanigans

Full Moon Shenanigans

Hotel Shenanigans

Dragon Shenanigans

Undercover Shenanigans

Spooky Shenanigans

Holiday Shenanigans

Valentine Shenanigans

Lucky Shenanigans

STORIES OF THE VEIL

Guardians of the Veil

Astra

Glory

Luna

Zara

Guardians of the Realms

WICKED

No Rest for the Wicked

Wicked Is As Wicked Does

Anthologies & Collections

MATCHMAKING CATS OF THE GODDESSES BUNDLES

The Cat's Meow

Holly Jolly Pawliday

Familiar Meowgic

The Devil's in the Cattails

SHENANIGANS ANTHOLOGIES

Crazed

Amazed

Holidazed

STORIES OF THE VEIL

The Unveiled

The Veiled

COMPLETE SERIES COLLECTIONS

Shenanigans

The Veil

Wicked

About the Author

PEPPER MCGRAW is a USA Today Bestselling Author of paranormal romance. Her life to date has sadly been paranormal-free, but she expects that will change in time. Until then, she keeps herself busy writing (and reading) paranormal romances.

Pepper loves animals, especially cats, and spends her free time volunteering at local shelters and for Trap-Neuter-Release programs. She's had the supreme honor of winning occasional head butts and meows from the community cats in her neighborhood and has even convinced a few to come inside and adopt her as their own.

amazon.com/author/peppermcgraw

bookbub.com/authors/pepper-mcgraw

facebook.com/ShenanigansSeries

goodreads.com/peppermcgraw

instagram.com/peppermcgraw_author

tiktok.com/@peppermcgraw

x.com/peppermcgraw